MORGAN'S LONG RIFLES

The long march to Quebec began. The cold and snow were setting in. Food and clothing were scarce. Some men were racked with illness because of toil and exposure. All were worn and ill-tempered.

This is the story of the battles at Quebec, Valcour Island, Freeman's Farm, Bemis Heights and Saratoga. And it is the story of the famous Revolutionary War soldiers—Daniel Morgan, Benedict Arnold, "Gentleman Johnny" Burgoyne—whose deeds are history.

Morgan's

Long Rifles

By Allan Taylor

Illustrated by Albert Orbaan

G. P. Putnam's Sons   New York

To Lois

Published simultaneously in the Dominion of
Canada by Longmans Canada Limited, Toronto
Library of Congress Catalog Card Number: 65–13306

MANUFACTURED IN THE UNITED STATES OF AMERICA
12216

CONTENTS

U. S. 1302757

MORGAN'S LONG RIFLES

I

FOR LIBERTY

A shot thudded from the enemy battery on the near side of Bunker Hill. It was quickly followed by others. Ben Donaldson and I halted, cuddling our rifleguns in our arms, and looked back. We had come up to high ground and could see both the smoke of the discharges and the bursts of the British mortar shells lofted at a new American entrenchment close to the Mystic River, near a mile from where we stood.

"Well sir, David Gordon," said Ben, in the way he had of using my full name when pleased about something. "Maybe we've pecked them into getting mad."

I watched the bursts. They were scattered and didn't seem to be doing much damage. "Into wasting more powder anyway," I replied. We had seen a lot of their shooting—both their short-range, high-arching bombshells and their solid shot and cannister—in the month since we had come to the siege lines around Boston, but it still surprised me that an army with so much artillery, which we lacked, used it so poorly.

9

Yet, in fairness, we knew nothing of artillery. What Ben and I knew and depended upon was the rifle, made for western hunters by skilled Pennsylvania gunsmiths. Its spirally grooved barrel, plus the greased patch of cloth around the bullet, made the bullet spin in flight, giving great precision, and accuracy up to 250 to 300 yards. This was at least twice the distance you could get with the generally used musket.

During that hot August afternoon we had been taking shots at the Redcoats on their line at the narrow neck of Charlestown peninsula. We hoped we had added to the respect the British were beginning to have for rifles shot by Virginians and Pennsylvanians who knew how to use them.

While we waited, Ben fished in his pocket for a rawhide string and tied it around one of his bead-bedecked, worn-out moccasins, which looked like decoration gone to ruin. "Seems we're going to have to fight this war barefoot," he observed, kicking the sole against the ground to make sure it wouldn't flap. I agreed, my own footgear being almost as bad.

Ben and I had been raised on neighboring farms near Winchester in Virginia. Because we had a rare understanding of and liking for each other, we would stand together against the world. It had been so since we were boys. I could recall only one scrap we'd had— at nine or ten it might have been—when we had basted each other for some reason long forgot and had ended a little bruised, respectful of each other and laughing at the ridiculousness of it all. We were, in effect, the closest of brothers, closer than many natural brothers.

We were seventeen, of about the same build and height, tall and wiry and physically hardened by our half-farmer, half-huntsman life in the Shenandoah Valley near the western edge of the Virginia settlements. Together we had volunteered for the company big, tough Daniel Morgan had been commissioned to raise by the Continental Congress after the war had started. Only half those who wanted to join had been chosen; the rest had been weeded out by a shooting match to see who was most skilled with a rifle.

For uniforms we wore long, gray hunting shirts fringed at the sleeves and skirt, homespun breeches, and leather leggings. We had powder horns slung to straps over our shoulders and a knife and a small tomahawk hatchet at our belts. On our round, brimmed hats was stitched the Patrick Henry motto, "Liberty or Death."

As to soldiering we were complete greenhorns. The company had been enlisted in a matter of ten days back in June. Almost at once we had started for the place of fighting up in Massachusetts. We had marched six hundred miles to Cambridge in three weeks, without losing a man. But the trip had been hard on moccasins, and a month of drilling and scouting under the stern command of General Washington had about finished them. And we had not been able to get shoes, for now, late in August 1775, there was still a scarcity of many things, even gunpowder, in our makeshift American army.

From this place we could see in the lengthening shadows of afternoon the two bits of land that were all the British now held of their rebellious New England colonies. Eastward was the Charlestown peninsula, with Bunker Hill its highest point. Near its end, at the mouth of the Charles River, was the burned wreckage of Charlestown. To the south, across the broad estuary of the Charles, was another peninsula from which rose three hills. Below the hills the ground was studded with the church spires and houses of Boston, the once busy seaport that had become a prison for the Redcoats.

The sight of Boston brought to mind the way the war had started in the spring. British troops had gone by night from Boston to seize arms their spies had learned the patriots were collecting to defend their rights against George III. Warned of the raid by a man named Revere and other riders who had slipped out of the town ahead of the troops, the farmers and townsmen of the colonial militia—Minutemen they called themselves—had turned out to fight.

There had been a skirmish at the villages of Lexington and Concord. As all the world knew, the British, surprised by the resistance and shot at from behind trees and rock fences, had pelted back.to Boston with faces as red as their coats, and militiamen had flocked from all New England to keep them penned there.

Two months later had come the fight on Charlestown peninsula, where the militia had labored through a night on breastworks with the idea of mounting cannons to command Boston. Next morning the British General Gage, seeing the danger but still contemptuous, had sent his regulars across the river. They had marched up bravely several times against the scanty fortifications but had been blasted back with heavy losses—so heavy that the lesson in Yankee courage seemed to have taken the starch out of the British army in Boston. At last, when their powder gave out, the New Englanders had retreated. But they were right proud of the Battle of Bunker Hill, as they had cause to be.

The bombardment slowed to a stop. We turned again toward camp. As we rounded a bend in the path I saw a figure approaching. Shading my eyes against the westering sun, I recognized the stocky frame and innocent-looking face of Jerry McGuire.

Jerry was of the Scotch-Irish people who had come to Pennsylvania, many staying there, others spreading down the mountain valleys of Virginia and Carolina. He was apt at any time to break out in a singsong stream of talk but, if need be, could stay as mum as a possum playing dead. He usually saw to it that the buttered side of the bread stayed up for Jerry McGuire. But he was loyal to his friends and was a good one to have around.

He greeted us with a burst of words. "It does seem now these New England folks is right sayin' the Redcoats couldn't hit a barn if they was inside it. When I first came to these parts the big Sassenach guns worried me, I'll admit, but not now." He drew his breath and added thoughtfully, "Still, if by chance one of them balls did smack you 'twould be good-bye Susie."

I had noticed by now that he was wearing new shoes in place of his battered moccasins. I asked him where he had gotten them.

"Shoes? Oh, these. Well now, let's see." His face was

blank but his brown eyes danced with laughter. "In Pennsylvany, or was it Jersey? With everybody hot after shoes and havin' to stay up nights guardin' 'em, it's hard to——."

"Now, now," drawled Ben, smiling in his slow sort of way, "stop the blather. You got them today."

Jerry grinned. "That I did, and I trotted up this hill to tell you afore the news gets around. 'Tis obleeged to me you should be, ye poltroons."

"Truly we are, your lordship," I minced. "Give out."

"Now that's better. Well—to make a long story short, while you were takin' shots at Redcoats I was finding out things. Passed the time of day with a Massachusetts man who'd bought a blanket from a sutler. Said he had shoes, too, but warned that the sutler, bein' a Connecticuter, would likely do me out of my shirt in a trade. Sounded like fun and I figured to risk it. That's the trouble, mind you, with this army. Everybody suspicions everybody outside their own province of bein' rascals—not that they ain't right half the time."

"That may be," I said patiently. "But about the sutler."

"I'm gettin' to that. Can't you let a man tell a thing his own way? Calls himself Honest Sam and butter wouldn't melt in his mouth. Two-tongued. Like the feller sellin' Injun Seneca oil for rheumatiz at two shillings the bottle. 'Brother,' says he, ' 'tis not the cost you should think about, 'tis the heaven-sent help it'll be a-curin' you.' "

"He may tell it by nightfall," sighed Ben.

But Jerry at last came out with it. "He has a tent and a wagon south of the river on the road to Roxbury where we've got the way to Boston blocked. About a mile and a half beyant the Charles, nigh to a settlement called Muddy River. A dumbhead couldn't miss it."

We walked down from this spur of Prospect Hill, which was a major strongpoint on the American lines stretching in a nine-mile semicircle around the land side of Boston. Passing between redoubts on the part of the line between the hill and the Charles River, we came in sight of our camp, a ramshackle collection of huts, tents, and leantos. Approaching it, we saw that something was wrong.

In front of the shelter a bunch of our men confronted a cluster of New Englanders who were shouting and waving their arms. Suddenly, as if by signal, the riflemen charged. In an instant the two groups merged into a fist-swinging mass.

As we raced toward the fight the familiar figure of a big man, tall and barrel-chested, stormed out of a hut. He went into action at once, laying about him with hamlike fists and bellowing oaths. He grabbed two men who were locked in a wrestle, tore them apart, and bashed their heads together. He knocked sprawling a fellow who tried to hit him with a piece of firewood. He bawled, "If you fools want to fight, fight the British." By the time we got there he had things under control, and the two groups had drawn gloweringly apart.

"That's Dan Morgan for ye," muttered Jerry admiringly.

The big man, red-faced, glared impartially at his own and at the others. "What's the meaning of this?" he demanded.

There was a moment of silence, then one of the

militiamen spoke up. "They stole a cut of beef from my tent." Another stoutly added: "We've no liking for your wild men lording it over law-abiding Massachusetts men. They're lazy troublemakers. Atop that, taking our vittals is too much."

Angry as he was, Morgan was fair-minded. Controlling his temper, he said: "Our western people 'listed to whip the British and they're restive. They're fighters and know it, and they give you credit for being the same. As for lawless," he added dryly, "we're all lawless or we wouldn't be rebelling against King and Parliament." He pointed at the first speaker. "Pick out the one who took your meat."

Jerry suddenly shrank behind me, kneeling and fumbling with his shoestrings.

The accuser hesitantly admitted that he had not seen the theft.

"Then how do you know a rifleman took it?" rumbled Morgan.

"They're always plundering."

"See you here, one of the first things to learn in an army is to guard your own," blatted Morgan. To the riflemen he growled, "Any of you I catch thieving will be flogged." To the Yankees he said in a calmer but authoritative tone: "Go back to your camp. No more brawling. We've got to stick together."

Muttering among themselves, the New Englanders slowly obeyed.

Jerry stood up and wiped sweat from his face. He met my stare solemnly. "Better get them shoes while they last," he said.

"So it was you?"

"I got around a lot today, Dave," he muttered. " 'Tis salt pork and stale bread we've been eating, and goin' almost footbare. They've got shoes and this morning they got a fresh-killed beef. They ought to share it. There's a piece hid away for us. Now you best leave the rifles in the hut. They'd only cumber you."

Smiling at Jerry's stratagems, Ben and I set off through the town of Cambridge, past the big red brick buildings of Harvard College, now being used as barracks, and the elm-shaded Common, overhung with bluish, pungent smoke from supper fires. At one side was Brattle Street, which housed the rich merchants. It was called Tory Row because some of the owners had sided with the British and had fled to Boston when war began. General Washington was using one of the mansions as headquarters.

We reached the causeway across a marsh which led to the bridge over the Charles. Here, above its broad stretch, the stream was narrow. Silently we took the road to Roxbury. The sun was setting but with the long twilight it would be a while until dusk.

My mind was on the fight at camp and Jerry's jabber about Americans being suspicious of each other. It was true. Many were still loyal to the King, some merely wanted grievances settled, and some were hot for independence. And many didn't care one way or the other. No wonder that General Washington, after taking command two months ago, had used harsh measures to forge the volunteers into a force able to stand against British regulars.

Farmers, their first anger past, who wanted to go

home to harvest crops. Malcontents who hated discipline. Washington needed more men like General Nathaniel Greene of Rhode Island, Colonel Benedict Arnold, who, with Ethan Allen's Green Mountain Boys, had captured Fort Ticonderoga on Lake Champlain—and, of course, Daniel Morgan.

As a youth Morgan had come to Virginia according to one account, after a quarrel with his father. By hard work and brains he had raised himself from day laborer to become the owner of a wagon train that freighted out wheat, hemp, and other products of the valley to the East Coast and brought back supplies needed by the settlers. He had been a wagoner with the young Washington's Virginia militia on the British General Braddock's disastrous march to the Forks of the Ohio in the French War.

Morgan had been a wild, scrappy one in his young years, hot-tempered and without schooling. But after he had gotten himself a wife and more or less settled down he had learned a good deal by reading. At length, he had become a prosperous farmer and respected leader in our western county of Frederick. Lately, he had added to his reputation in the war Lord Dunmore, Governor of Virginia, had waged against the Shawnee Indians of the Ohio.

Morgan was forty, but the men in his company, mostly much younger, called him "the Old Wagoner" and sometimes "Dirty Dan." In truth, we had much rougher names for him too, for he was a hard and driving man. Yet we highly respected him and, indeed, had an odd sort of affection for him.

Against the British he held a personal grudge. Years

earlier, as an army wagoner, he had struck an over-bearing officer. He had been sentenced to 500 lashes with a bullwhip—enough to kill some men. His back still bore the scars and at times when he went shirtless in the woods, Indian-fashion, and people noted them, he would grimly joke that the British owed him another lick; the drummer whose duty it was to inflict the punishment had lost count and stopped at 499. It was typical of Morgan that he *hadn't* lost count.

There was still a good deal of light when we reached the place we were seeking. A tent was pitched near the road. Beside it stood two horses tied to a covered wagon. Another horse grazed nearby. Noiselessly we crossed the grass toward the tent.

We were near the entrance when we heard a voice from inside. It sounded raspy and urgent. The accent puzzled me; it wasn't New England and it wasn't quite British. We caught the words: "This is much more important than a powder shortage. Read it."

We stopped, I suppose because this seemed a private talk. But we were near enough to hear what followed. There was a rustle of paper, then a low whistle of surprise.

"A daring thing," exclaimed a deeper voice. "By all accounts they choose a hard road."

"But they might possibly succeed," said the other voice. "If they do, there's nothing up there at present to keep them from taking it. This must get to Gage tonight. See to it after dark. Now I must go."

Ben and I took a couple of quick steps backward. We did it instinctively, for something here seemed wrong. What was wrong was the name "Gage." It was the name of the British general in command in Boston.

A man came out of the tent. He halted quickly at sight of us. We saw him clearly. He wore good clothes —a blue coat with lace at the sleeves, a fancy neck-cloth, a large tricorn hat. His face was thin and taut, with a large hawklike nose. His rather full lips didn't go with the rest of the countenance. His cold gray eyes were very sharp.

"What do you want here, young riflemen?" he demanded.

"Shoes," said I curtly, not liking his looks or manner.

He glanced at our moccasins, then asked if we had been waiting long.

"Just got here," said Ben, which was near enough true.

He gave us another searching look, then, seeming to make up his mind, he called: "Samuel, two customers for shoes."

A large bearlike man in a brown smock came out of the tent. After a quick glance at the other, he looked us over. On the left cheek of his roundish face was the scar of an old knife wound. He was thickset, but muscular rather than fat. He stuck out a hand to shake first mine and then Ben's. I noticed he did it with an odd hunching of shoulders and forward thrust of his head, but paid little mind to it at the time because it was a small thing, so to speak.

"Samuel Winter is the name," he said heartily, as if real pleased to meet us. "Known everywhere as Honest

Sam. If it's shoes you want, it's shoes you'll get—unless your feet are mismated." He gave a kind of laugh and added, "Good patriots ought to help our boys all they can." He went to the wagon, drew up part of the canvas covering, and tossed out a batch of shoes to try on for size.

The other man stood watching in the fading light until Ben and I found pairs that fitted and bought them with shillings left from our last pay day. Then he mounted his horse. As we started back toward Cambridge Ben pulled his left ear in our sign for caution. Behind us we heard the mounted man say: "I'm on my way. I'll help with that business deal, if necessary." Darting a glance back, I saw him spur away to the south on the Roxbury road.

We walked until we were out of view from the meadow, then ducked into the woods to talk.

"Some kind of flapdoodle back there," muttered Ben.

It seemed very likely. The two were not what they wanted us to think them. They suspected we had overheard their words in the tent. Whatever enterprise they were up to was to start after dark. The message to Gage—was it actually for the British general? There was much talk of Tories spying for the Redcoats. And yet it might be something else entirely.

Ben was for going back and tackling the sutler to get the message. It was a tempting idea, but I felt that we should find out more. And if Boston really was his aim, I was curious to see how he would try to get there. It was said that we had strong works near Roxbury at the

narrow neck of marshland connecting Boston with the
mainland. He might have a boat hidden along the river
above the Neck, but there were some American outposts there, too. The upshot was that we decided to
wait until dusk deepened, then return to the meadow
to see what would happen.

It was nearing full dark when we crept back to the
edge of the meadow. A candle was burning in the tent.
We had hardly settled to watch when it went out and
the sutler emerged, a dim bulk in the faint afterglow
from the west. The horses whinnied hungrily as he
passed, crossed the road, and took to an open field. He
seemed to be avoiding the settlement called Muddy

River that began down the road a piece. We went after him.

The night was a poor one for trailing, for the moon would not rise until the small hours of morning and starlight isn't much to go by. However, in the open we at least had that, and by keeping within fifty or sixty feet of our man we could make him out. In this fashion we followed for what I judged to be nearly two miles, part of the time with lights from the village houses on our right. At length, he hit the road again, crossed a bridge over a stream, and soon after turned off into a thick, swampy growth of dwarf trees and was swallowed by blackness.

Luckily we could follow him by the sounds of his stumblings and threshings. After perhaps a half hour of this we were suddenly out of the woods into marsh reeds on a tidal flat near the river. To our right, somewhat behind us, were a few dim lights from another settlement.

The man cautiously made his way through the tall marsh grass, stopping now and then as if to listen or to fix his position. I was bemused. If the dim lights were from houses in Roxbury, as I suspected, we must be near the Neck. But where were the redoubts and the militia guards? Had we somehow slipped around them?

The answer came quickly. A voice nearby cried, "Halt! Where d'ye think you're—" and stopped short. Another, farther away, called out nervously, "What's going on here?" A sound of swishing, as of men running, then a rattle of musket shots.

At the first sound the sutler was in motion. We bounded after him, knowing now that we had to get him before he reached the British line. For a big man he was speedy. It seemed a long time before we closed the gap. We were within two jumps of him when he heard us and whirled. "Help!" he bawled. "King's soldiers. Help!"

We hit him together. The three of us went down on the mucky ground in a writhing, struggling mass. He was strong as a bull, and even as he fought he kept shouting for help. It was in my mind to stun him with the flat of my tomahawk and drag him back to our line, but as I grasped the tomahawk there was a rush of feet behind us.

"There they are. Grab them."

To my amazement the voice was that of the man in the blue coat.

Ben sprang up. "Run for it," he gasped.

I pried myself from the sutler's grip. As I got free a musket butt struck me. The blow glanced off my shoulder before it hit my head else my skull would have been cracked. As it was, I went down, dazed.

The next thing I knew I was jerked to my feet, with two men grasping my arms, and a lantern, held high by a Redcoat, shining in my face.

"Better dispose of him," snapped Blue Coat. "Knows too much."

Out of a babble of voices someone said in a clipped British accent: "We can't do that. He's a prisoner." More buzzings of voices—or were they inside my head? What happened next remains a blur. Giddy and sick, I fought for consciousness. The two who held me must have half-dragged, half-carried me.

Dancing lanterns. A bridge over a moat. Entrenchments. Cannon. A road, with a lantern-bearer going ahead. A brick wall with an arched gateway. Finally a sort of stable, with a cow in a stall. Despite my struggles, they bound me hand and foot and propped me, sitting, against a wall. The man with the lantern set it down and left.

All of this must have taken place quickly, for there was another burst of firing in the distance. One of the Redcoats cocked his ear at the sound. "I'm going back there, Tucker," he told the other. "Watch him. Careful now."

"No fear, Sergeant," replied the man. He seated himself on a milking stool facing me, with his back to the open end of the shed.

Minutes passed. The firing stopped. My throbbing head was full of confused thoughts. Had Ben escaped? What could I do now? I wriggled my wrists, trying the bindings, and winced at the pain in my shoulder.

"None o' that," warned the Redcoat. He pointed his musket at me.

It was then that I saw a figure, dim in the lantern light, move cautiously into view at the open end of the shed. The man stood a moment, taking in the scene, then raised a finger to his lips for silence. In his other hand was a stout cudgel. I looked as blank as I could manage, showing no surprise lest the soldier sense someone was behind him.

The stranger tiptoed slowly, with infinite caution, toward the guard. I coughed and wriggled again to hold the soldier's attention. The man struck. The club hit the Redcoat on the side of his head. He toppled over without a sound.

The stranger was beside me. He used my knife to cut my bonds. He blew out the lantern. "Can you walk?" he asked.

"Yes."

"Then come. Trust me and keep quiet. There's no time to lose."

2

ESCAPE FROM BOSTON

We slipped into a road lined with houses which were separated by intervals of open space. Lights shone from some of them. I sensed that we were still on a narrow neck of land. I stumbled and the stranger gripped my arm. He was silent and tense.

There was good reason for his worry, for soon two lanterns appeared ahead of us. By their glow I could see the scarlet coats, white breeches, and black gaiters of a British patrol. We ducked into a path and hid in marsh grass behind a house.

When the patrol passed, the stranger got up and peeled off his coat. "Put this on," he whispered. "In that shirt anybody would know you for an American Ranger. Lost your hat in the rumpus, I see. Just as well. Take off those leggings and hide them under the coat."

I obeyed. My head was aching and my shoulder throbbed with pain, but the shock had passed and, while it was evident that this man meant me well, I was curious. "What is your aim?"

"To get you out of Boston."

While I was being dragged to the stable I had thought of Ben, wondering if he had escaped, fearing that he had not. Now, out of strong feeling, I spoke louder than I should have. "But Ben—my friend—he was with me. I've got to know if they caught him. If they did, maybe we can get him away."

The man's grip on my arm tightened. "Sh-h-h. No time or place for talking." He led through the tall grass until we came to a lane which soon turned at right angle. At length we passed a block of closely built houses. After another turn we came to a path between two rows of trees in what seemed a large open space.

"Boston Common," my guide explained. "Less chance of trouble here, but talk low. How did you get into this fix?"

I told him of the sutler and his partner in the blue coat, of why we had followed the sutler and of how I had been captured. I was amazed at it all, and ashamed of our part in it. Ben and I deemed ourselves good at scouting; we had sensed that Blue Coat was suspicious; yet we had walked into his trap like fools.

I recalled his words to the sutler, his promise to "help in that business deal." That should have warned us. He had gone immediately to get help to see that the message got to Boston. Judging by the sounds, he and his Tories had even been bold enough to knock out an American sentry.

"Bad luck," said my companion charitably. "They couldn't have done it by daylight. The Roxbury redoubts firesweep most of that end of the Neck, and guards cover the rest. Even on a night like this your

Tories must have kept close to the edge of the river. And now what of this friend of yours?"

"I don't know. That's why I want to go back. I don't see how he could have got away. They were on top of us."

He halted and pondered the matter. "Still, he might have," he said. "As long as they didn't nab both of you instanter there's a fair chance of it. No, going back is too risky."

"But we must," I urged.

"See here, young fellow," he said with a touch of impatience, "we'd be stark mad to go back there now with the Redcoats looking for you and watching every move hereabouts. It was pure luck I was able to free you."

Torn between worry over Ben and gratitude to this man who had taken a dangerous chance to help me, I said: "Sir, I am much beholden to you. What is your name?"

He didn't answer for a moment and when he did his tone told me he was amused. "Just call me Johnny-Go-Between. That's my work." For all that, he was sympathetic. "I'll make inquiries. If they've got your friend —and that's not at all certain—I'll try to find him, though it would be a large order. But *you* I can get out now. If you don't come with me you'll likely spend years in a British prison."

His low voice was impassioned. "Listen to me. We need every man in the colonies, but especially we need you riflemen. Our boys at Bunker Hill had the right idea, taking shelter and shooting 'em before they could get close. But you boys can do it better. You can beat their blasted volleys and bay'net charges."

He paused, then added quietly: "I have a boat. It's a good mile and a half to it, most of the way right through town. We'll stroll along, minding our business. If anything happens we'll run for it."

Soon we left the Common and came into a street lined with small houses. Few people were abroad, for Boston had lost half its population, with patriots having moved out to towns behind our lines. We met a few off-duty soldiers but they paid us no attention. Making still another turn, we entered a broader street faced by houses of two and three stories and better lighted than the one we had left.

After a bit we came into a small square and approached a house which, by the talk and laughter heard through its open door, seemed to be a tavern. Here, we came near to disaster. As we were about to pass the door two young British officers tumbled out. One, bad gone in his cups, was cursing his luck at cards. The other was trying to support and calm his lurching companion. As we sought to slip by, he told the other: "Early in the night as it is, you're fuddled, Walmsley, you've had enough."

The drunk one tore loose from his friend's grasp and before I could jump out of the way staggered against me. He rebounded, stared blearily, muttered, "Demmed rebel scum," and aimed a wild blow at me. I side-stepped, and tripped him into the gutter. My guide grabbed me by the hand and leaped toward a dark alley leading off the square. Behind us the other officer yelped shrilly for the guard.

We ducked and dodged until we shook off pursuit.
At last we came into a triangular open space. On its far
side a building topped with a steeple was vaguely dis-
cernible in the gloom.

"Old North Church," muttered my companion.
"We'll soon be there. See those lights to our right?
That's the long wharf," he said with a touch of pride.

At a considerable distance across a blackness I took
to be water, I could see, faint as stars, a long line of
lights stretching out into the harbor. The wharf was
said to be the greatest ship pier in the colonies. A
Boston militiaman had boasted of the ships that had
brought to it tea from India, woolens from England,
sugar from the West Indies. That was over, of course,
but the British kept lights on it for their own reasons.

After some minutes of groping along a narrow street
we went down a short slope onto an unlighted dock. I
heard the soft lapping of wavelets. My guide whispered
a warning; there was a sentry hereabouts. He felt his
way to one of the dock's pilings, said the boat was beneath, and directed me to follow him. He clutched the
piling and slid down it.

Several things happened simultaneously. I heard a
rattling sound from below, followed by a thump. There
were footsteps on the dock. I slipped over the edge but,
uncertain of what lay below, froze to the piling, hoping
I was invisible.

" 'Oo's there?" challenged a booming voice. A
pause. " 'Ere, wot's 'appening, I say? Speak up, you."

A hand caught my foot. I slid down into a rowboat
that rocked gently on the incoming tide. The sentry

thumped about overhead, swearing at the "blasted blackness." Sometime later he gave up and went away.

"Blamed thing wasn't where I thought," complained my companion. "Tide had swept it." He waited for what seemed an age before he untied the boat, placed the oars and pushed off.

He rowed slowly and very quietly around the end of the Boston peninsula and into the mouth of the Charles. As he headed up the broad estuary the riding lights of the British ships that at times cannonaded our entrenchments were around us. He wormed his way between them, giving a wide berth to the big *Somerset*, where a careful watch would be kept. When the last of the vessels was well astern he quickened his stroke. "We can talk now," he said. "Tell me more about these fellows."

Marshaling the impressions in my aching head, I described the sutler and his partner in more detail and repeated the words we had overheard, which I had not told him before. He was silently thoughtful for a time. "I must try to find out what that message means," he muttered.

"When I reach camp I'll get help and we'll grab the sutler. He's bound to come back for his team and wagon."

He agreed that this seemed my best tack.

It was then that I asked a question I had been thinking of ever since his first dramatic appearance—how he had happened to be at the right spot at the right time to knock out my guard.

My companion laughed. "To begin with, there's

some of us loyal subjects of King George that make a habit of walking the streets nights sort of looking things over and picking up bits when we can. Tonight —for special reasons—I was at that end of town. Close enough to the gate in the wall at the Neck to see them pulling you toward that cowshed. That was the part that was luck. It was plain you were an American prisoner. When the shooting started and the sergeant went back I saw my chance and took it."

It was a daring thing, and again I tried to thank him, but he shrugged it off. Nor would he tell anything more about his activities.

The river narrowed as we neared Cambridge. Some distance short of town the man headed the boat toward shore. "It's not far now," he said. "I must be back in Boston and off the streets before moonrise."

The bow touched land. I gave back the coat and put on my leggings. The man who called himself Johnny-Go-Between shook hands warmly and promised to send news of Ben if he could get any.

I felt my way past some farm houses and through an apple orchard to a place on the lines where I was fairly sure of slipping in without being challenged. It took about half an hour to reach the hut I shared with five others.

At the entrance I stopped, and into my still muddled head came the fancy that all of this was a bad dream— that I might soon wake up and find Ben asleep on his pallet. But no, it was real. Entering, I groped for Ben's sleeping place. My hand touched an empty blanket. I found Jerry and prodded him. He sprang up with an exclamation, then, reassured, gasped, "So 'tis you, praise be. Is Ben with you?"

I told him that I had hoped to find Ben here.

"He's not."

Jerry struck sparks from a flint and from the glowing tinder lighted a candle. The others were now awake. "Real glad to see you," said Solomon Binns, the oldest of my hutmates. William Riddle and Peter Anderson sat up, rubbing their eyes. Riddle grumpily wanted to know what was the matter. I told them. When I had finished Jerry spoke.

"Well, now. This time we'll wait for that sutler if it takes a week."

It came to me that I was hungry, so I reached into my haversack, got a piece of hardbread and a slice of meat, and took a drink from the wooden canteen hanging on a wall peg. I was at work on the bread and meat when it occurred to me to ask what Jerry meant by "this time."

For once he got quickly to the point. Some two hours after dark, prompted perhaps by an instinct about the sutler, he had begun to wonder at our absence. An hour later he and Solomon had decided to investigate. Leaving the others asleep, they had gone to the sutler's camp. The tent, the horses, and the wagon were there, but no sutler. They had waited for a time, then, baffled, had come back.

"How long ago was that?" I demanded.

Solomon stepped outside and looked at the stars. "Little over an hour," he replied. "It's nigh onto one o'clock now." It was known he could tell time rather accurately at night by the stars, a thing many on the frontier could do more or less well, but he was better than most because he had practiced it when he was fighting Shawnees in the Ohio country.

"Let's go," I said.

We picked up our rifles. Jerry blew out the candle. We circled the center of town to avoid sentries, reached the bridge, and took the road to Roxbury. It was slow going in the blackness, but at last we neared the familiar meadow and stopped to plan our course. If the sutler had come back, he might be either in the tent or in the wagon. Three would go for the tent, two for the wagon. If he wasn't there, we would wait.

Braced for action, we came to the edge of the open space, peered into it. Not trusting my eyes, I strode into the meadow. To make sure, we crisscrossed it carefully.

It was empty. The sutler, with his tent and his wagon, had vanished.

3

THE SECRET PLAN

Late in the morning I came out of sleep with a sunbeam blazing on my face. I was alone, the others having gone to drill or shoot at the British or whatever they were about. I felt dull and of no account.

We had returned to camp as the moon rose. I had sunk into a sleep filled with dreams of a man in a blue coat who suddenly turned into a huge, fierce hawk, and of a creature with the head of a man and the body of a bear who threw shoes at me. Later I must have fallen into deep slumber.

It was another hot, sun-drenched day. I went to the barrel of water that stood under a nearby tree, doused a gourdful over my head, and washed my face and hands in the wooden trencher beside the barrel. I was tenderly feeling the lump on my head when I saw Lieutenant William Heath approaching.

"You all right?" he asked.

"I'm fit," I replied shortly, not wishing to talk.

"Had anything to eat?"

"Ate a few hours ago but I could do with more."

"Then you'd best grab something and chew as you go. The Captain wants to see you. He's with Colonel Benedict Arnold at General Washington's headquarters."

This was bad news. "What does he want?" I asked.

"He's heard what happened to you and Ben Donaldson last night. But why that's big enough stuff to haul you before the General is beyond me."

Low in spirit, I followed Heath into town, past the Common and on to the mansion occupied by General Washington and his staff. At the door a sentry smartly saluted Heath and asked our business. After Heath's reply the sentry called an orderly to fetch an officer and then froze into a statue, looking as stiff and brainless as a wooden toy. Clearly, discipline was demanded here.

An aide appeared—a supercilious young man wearing a long silver-buttoned coat and fancy waistcoat. The queue of his powdered hair was tightly bound in eelskin. He was a real dandy. He motioned us into a hall and bade us wait, saying that Colonel Arnold and Captain Morgan were in conference with the Commander.

Heath, disdaining such fuss and feathers, started softly whistling a tune.

Arnold's name was now widely known, for he was rapidly gaining fame in the army. It was said that as a mere lad he had run a business in New Haven, Connecticut. Later, he had owned ships that traded with Canada, the West Indies, and Europe. In his twenties he had grown fairly well-to-do and now, at thirty-four, he was determined to make a reputation in the war.

With Ethan Allen he had ably carried out the capture of Fort Ticonderoga on Lake Champlain, with its badly needed cannon. He was said to be absolutely fearless.

While I was turning over in my mind what to say and wondering about the outcome, a man in a handsome uniform appeared from a room at the rear of the hall. He was a bit shorter than average. His face was reddish and lined, his hair graying and scraggly, and he wore spectacles perched on the hook of his big nose. I knew him to be Horatio Gates, a former British officer who a few years before had sold his commission in an army where preferences and promotions usually went to rich young lordlings rather than to men of ordinary birth. He had come to America and settled on land in the Shenandoah north of Winchester. He knew Daniel Morgan and liked him. Now he was General Washington's chief of staff with the rank of brigadier general.

"You are leaving now?" he said to someone behind him.

"Immediately, sir," replied a voice that seemed somehow familiar. "My horse is saddled and waiting. By hard riding I hope to overtake General Schuyler at the upper end of Champlain."

"Don't you want to see Colonel Arnold?"

"It is not necessary, sir. He knows the need for haste."

As he passed the bench I saw his face and was struck dumb. I stared in gape-mouthed amazement, scarcely believing my eyes. But it was true; there couldn't be two so exactly alike. He was the hawk-nosed man of the tent, the spy who had been our undoing in the black marshes of Boston Neck. He was wearing different clothes now, a dun-colored jacket and riding boots, but the face was unmistakably the same. He reached the door, saluted, and strode rapidly away.

I sprang up after him, but Heath caught my arm. "What's the matter with you?"

"That fellow," I gasped. "He's a spy. He sent the message."

"Rubbish. You're dreaming."

"I'm not," I fairly shouted. "I swear it. He mustn't get away."

Suddenly we were interrupted. "Here, what is this uproar about?" General Gates, on his way back to his office, was peering nearsightedly at me.

"General, sir, who was that man with you?" I blurted.

"What are you doing here?" he asked coldly.

"Captain Morgan sent for him, sir," replied Heath.

"Captain Morgan, eh? Ahem, yes. I have a high regard for him. Why did he send for you?"

"I reckon it's about last night."

I began to explain, then hesitated, for even in my excitement I realized that I could easily get into deep water. Choosing words carefully, I gave him a bare outline of what had happened. His stare grew more and more incredulous as I went on.

"Young man, is this make-believe?" he queried sternly.

"No, sir. It happened. That man is a British spy." I made the charge regardless of result, thinking that by now I might as well be hung for a sheep as for a lamb.

Gates looked at Heath. "My, my, this is a most serious charge against one who has Colonel Arnold's trust. What do you have to do with it?"

"Nothing, sir. I wasn't there." Heath paused, then thought better of it and went on. "But, General, this lad is no harum-scarum. If he says it's so it's worth looking into."

Gates regarded me through narrowed eyes, rubbing his nose thoughtfully. "Perhaps it is," he murmured. "For your sake, young man, I truly hope you are not using your imagination to cover some escapade." He rapped on a door across the hall and entered.

Heath muttered that I was truly in the frying pan now, a statement I was in no mood to dispute. In a few moments the door opened and Gates beckoned us in.

As I crossed the threshold I was conscious of three pairs of eyes watching me, and of three varying expressions. Big Dan looked grim. Seated at his right was a stocky man, with swarthy complexion, bold blue eyes, long thin nose, and domineering chin. He wore the uniform of the Governor's Footguards of New Haven—scarlet coat, with buff collar, lapels, and cuffs, white breeches and stockings, and black half-leggings. Colonel Benedict Arnold. I darted a glance at the third figure, a big-framed man in a dark-blue coat with buff facings who sat behind a desk. General Washington's large, rugged face, somewhat pitted by smallpox he had had as a youth, was impassive. His gaze was coolly appraising.

Morgan spoke first. "Gordon, I heard what happened to you from McGuire. It sounded as if you'd hit on something that might be important right now. I sent for you so you could tell the General. And now, only this minute, you say one of your spies is Colonel Arnold's friend. Have you gone lightheaded? What's it about?"

"It's stupid," broke in Arnold in a rather high-pitched voice. "Why waste time on fables?"

"Let's hear the story," said Washington.

I drew a deep breath. My knees were shaking. As I launched into the tale of misadventure Washington and Morgan listened intently. Arnold frowned and fidgeted in a manner to bear out his reputation as a man of great vigor and ambition, restless, and impatient of obstacles.

When I told of the message being given to the sutler Arnold interrupted, wanting to know the gist of it. I replied, of course, that I didn't know but that Ben and I had heard enough to be suspicious, and that if it was going to the British we wanted to stop it.

"Repeat exactly what you overheard," directed Washington.

Prodding my memory, I told of the words about a powder shortage as we came up, then of the paper being passed to the sutler and the sutler's whistle as he read it. "The sutler said, 'They choose a hard road,' " I continued. "Then this other man, the one who was here just now, said, 'But they might possibly succeed. If they do, there's nothing up there at present to keep them from taking it.' That was why he wanted the message to get to Gage fast."

"This is sheer—" began Arnold.

"Gently, Colonel," interrupted Washington. To me

he said: "When you heard the words 'nothing up there at present to keep them from taking it,' did 'up there' and 'it' mean anything to you?"

I replied that they hadn't, that what worried us was the name Gage—and the way the man had acted when he found us outside the tent.

"Go on."

Quickly I told of the ambush, the rescue, and the sutler's disappearance.

Arnold smiled and shrugged. Abruptly he got up and began pacing back and forth in front of Morgan. "Idiotic," he barked. "George Tremaine is a patriot." He swung to face me. "This happened, you say, at dusk. How could you be sure of a face then?"

"It started before dusk, sir. There was still plenty of light."

"Describe this man."

I did so, stressing the unusual features of his face.

"That's not a very good picture of Tremaine," objected Arnold.

"But it is a fair description of the man who was here a few minutes ago," said Gates in a precise, schoolmasterish manner. "On your recommendation Tremaine was accepted as trustworthy. But I had never seen him before and he is carrying important dispatches to Schuyler. His credentials seemed all right, but just who is he, Colonel Arnold?"

Arnold glared. "He is known to me through business dealings in Jamaica. He is devoted to our cause. Come, come, sirs. A way to check this tale is to find the man he says got him out of Boston. I'll wager you won't."

"Inquiries will be made," replied Gates stiffly.

Big Dan had been gazing at the ceiling. "Colonel," he said, "with all respect for your judgement, it's just possible this lad is not mistaken in his man. It might even be that the fellow he's talking about isn't Tremaine at all."

It was then that Arnold showed his quickness of mind. He sat down, chin in hand, brooding. "That would be devilishly daring," he muttered. "Tremaine was scheduled to leave today with dispatches for Schuyler. If he has left without seeing me it would be odd but no more, in view of his haste. All right, I don't believe any of this, but I suggest, General Washington, that a courier be dispatched to the Champlain expedition as a precaution."

Washington nodded. He brushed a large hand across his forehead as if to sweep away other problems to deal with this new one.

"The plan may be known," he observed. "This may be a mistake of identity, but the account impressed me as a straight one, whoever the traitor is. They have known of our move on Montreal. They have not known more, but now they may. All the more reason for haste."

"We should have been off a week ago," grumbled Arnold.

A gloomy silence followed. Washington, whose broad shoulders bore heavy responsibilities in this war on the British Crown, drummed his fingers on the desk. Suddenly he flashed me a smile that transformed his austere features. "You may go now," he said. "Don't repeat what you have heard here. Not to anyone."

So this was the harsh Washington, the terror of militiamen! To me he seemed a great, self-controlled, gracious man, and, outside, I said so to Heath.

"Seems you did all right with him. Lucky. I wouldn't want to cross him. He knows what he's doing, but he's got a hard row to hoe what with trying to make an army out of a bunch of farmers and get what he needs from the tightfisted Congress."

On the way back to camp I mulled over the whole fantastic affair. And the more I thought about it, the fishier some things about it seemed.

A week passed, a week of heavy rainstorms, one following another after a brief interval of sunshine. I began to feel that the rain god, whether of the Indians or the Pluvius of the Romans, had a personal grudge against us. There had been no news of Ben from Johnny-Go-Between. Guards at Roxbury had vouched for my story of a disturbance that night, but they had seen nothing of Ben. This was agonizing. It meant that he had either been killed or captured.

As the days passed tempers had gotten on edge. And in spite of the downpours there were more drills than ever.

Daniel Morgan had something on his mind. He worked us remorselessly. Sometimes, because it was required, the drill was the formal European close-order one which tries to turn men into machines. We were poor at it and disliked it. So did Morgan, who blamed such tactics for Braddock's defeat. Granting the need for that kind of disciplined fighting, it was up to Washington and the drillmasters to develop it. Morgan himself had other notions about light infantry, and especially about riflemen.

His was a new idea about the standard book-taught war tactics of the times. It was based on mobility, elusiveness, surprise. It was aimed at inflicting the greatest damage on the other fellow at the least cost to ourselves.

He would take us into the woods and meadows back of the lines, point out the position of an imaginary enemy, and tell us what the enemy was trying to do. There was no shooting, for powder and ball were scarce, but we'd take cover and click firelocks from behind trees or up in the branches, and work around the enemy.

It was much like fighting Indians except that Indians don't stand up in a line and pour volleys at you and then charge with bayonets. That was what we had to get used to, and learn to lick. He would bawl directions, telling us to retreat at one point, advance at another, and rally us to him with gobbles from a turkey call he kept in his pocket. After it was over, if he wasn't satisfied he would blister us with criticisms.

His ideas were based on the rifle's great advantage, its range and true aim; on its disadvantage, the time it took to reload—and on our self-reliance and ability to take care of ourselves alone or in small groups.

"You've got to spread out and keep cover," he would repeat again and again. "Take good aim and sting 'em like hornets. Pick off the officers, artillerymen, horses, but don't try to stand against volleys or charges. You get killed that way. Fall back and start peckin' 'em again. Take 'em from a new quarter. Keep eternally thinning 'em down until they're ready to quit. And listen for the turkey call and do what I say."

One night after a day of such practice I was greasing my rifle against rust. The others in the hut were playing cards when someone outside the hut called my name. I got up and went out.

Caleb

A figure in the darkness said: "Come away a bit. I want to talk with you."

The flat, nasal tone was familiar but I couldn't place it. "Who are you?" I asked.

The man chuckled and said: "Seeing me only once in the light, I don't blame you." Then I knew.

"Johnny-Go-Between!" I exclaimed.

"I was," he corrected. "But no use hiding my name now. I'm called Caleb Perkins."

My first thought was of Ben. Had he been found?

"Yes, I found him—but too late," said the other. "He was captured as you thought. Took me several days to get trace of him. Before I could do anything more he was put aboard ship with some other prisoners. No chance of freeing him; they were kept in irons under heavy guard."

This was a blow, but at least Ben was alive. "We could get boats," I said. "The whole company would come. We could take the ship at night."

"Then you'd have to get away without rousing the fleet," he replied. "Anyway it's too late. The ship sailed yesterday."

"To England?"

"No, to Canada. Way I heard it, most of the prisoners will be held at Halifax in Nova Scotia, but some will go on to Quebec."

To me, either place seemed as hopeless as the Tower of London. "Then he may never get away," I muttered.

"Chances are he won't, at least for quite a time. But it might depend on where they take him."

"What do you mean?"

"Nothing. Just an idea." ˙

And that was all I could get out of him. I did, however, learn that in trying to locate Ben, Caleb Perkins, alias Johnny-Go-Between, had used up his luck. The British had got wind of what he was doing. He had escaped just in time. After saying this he fell silent, though I sensed there was something else on his mind. After a time, he awkwardly came out with it.

"Since I can't help in Boston anymore, it's time for me to join up," he said. "What I'd like would be to enlist with you riflemen."

It was a surprising idea but, as I thought about it, it seemed a good one. I said we would see Morgan.

Big Dan was sitting on a three-legged stool before a wooden box that he used as a desk. By the light of a candle he was laboriously writing a letter. He scowled at the interruption, but when I told him who Caleb was his manner changed.

"So you're the one who got Gordon out of town. We've been looking for you."

"Yes, sir. Sort of hard to believe it happened that way," replied Caleb shrewdly.

Morgan said that it was good work and that he was glad to have the story confirmed.

"Captain, the British know about him now and he can't go back," I said. "So he wants to join up with us."

Big Dan's face went blank. "You a Boston man?" he drawled.

"That I am."

Morgan shook his head morosely. "I warn you, I'm a hard man to please. You'd like it better with your New England folks."

Caleb was ready with an answer. "I want to fight with your riflemen. I calculate you've got a good way to beat those lobsterbacks." He winked solemnly and added: "Besides, where you're going it mightn't be a bad thing to have a man along who knows boats."

Morgan darted a suspicious glance at me, though Caleb's remark baffled me. He seemed about to say something, but thought better of it. He regarded Caleb keenly for a moment, then grunted, "All right." And so it was arranged.

Caleb came back to the hut. The card game was abandoned and Jerry and the others began questioning him about himself, where he had come from, what he had been doing. But their curiosity got little satisfaction, for Caleb had asked me not to tell them just yet, and he himself was adept at the answer that said nothing.

During the next few days there were signs of something unusual afoot. Morgan made a careful inspection of rifles and equipment. We drew a month's pay, amounting to forty shillings for privates. A sutler arrived with shoes, moccasins, and other needful things. Warmer clothing was issued, which seemed strange as it was early September and still hot.

Naturally, there were rumors. It was said we were to storm Boston, though just how this would be done was not clear. Some thought we were going west to protect settlements from British-led Indians. Soon the real plan was known. It was Jerry, of course, who first heard the news. He burst excitedly into the hut.

"Now I know why Dirty Dan has been tryin' to plumb ruin us with all his drillin' and traipsin' around and shinnyin' up trees," he proclaimed. "Never a word of the truth from him."

"So what is it?" This from Riddle.

"A bit of talk I've been having with the Rhode

Islanders of Captain Thayer's Company. They're 'listing men to fill their rolls for where we're goin'. Through terrible country, they say. Only a few Injuns ever make the trip."

"Wherever an Injun can go—" began Solomon indignantly. But Jerry was too intent on his revelations to brook an interruption.

" 'T'is an odd thing we weren't told first, since we're leading the way," he rambled on. "Dirty Dan kept this from us and I had to hear it from strangers. That's not right at all, at all."

Caleb was grinning. For an instant I wondered why, then, remembering what he had said to Morgan about going somewhere and having a man along who knew boats, I understood. "You've known, too, Caleb," I charged.

"Yep," he admitted placidly. "And if this young fellow doesn't get around to the point soon, I will. It's time now to tell."

Jerry stared at him. "Why, you—you codfish," he exclaimed. "All right," he added hastily, "it's Quebec. We're going up through woods in a place they call Maine and on to Canady. There ain't any Redcoats at Quebec now. What few there was have been sent to Montreal to hold it against our boys coming up from the lake. If we can get there fast—." He paused and rubbed his tousled brown hair thoughtfully. "But they say it's rough going."

All was suddenly clear. The message to Gage. The talk at Washington's headquarters. I remembered what my father had told me of the French and Indian War, of how, by winning the decisive battle at the fortress of Quebec in 1759, the British had gained in the following year, Canada and all the vast country west of the mountains to the Mississippi, the country of the Ohio and the Big Lakes which a few French fur traders had held in the name of their King. Now the Continental Congress and General Washington hoped to take Quebec, the city on the rock, and the fur-trading town of Montreal. If they could, we would gain a wilderness empire. At last the words "hard road" and "there's nothing up there at present to keep them from taking it" had meaning.

Jerry continued to unload his news. Benedict Arnold would lead us. Most of the force would be from New England, ten companies of musket men. Besides Morgan's company there would be two other rifle companies from Pennsylvania under Captain Hendricks and Captain Smith. Boats were being built on a river called the Kennebec to help us get to Canada.

This set me to thinking about Arnold. I had been against him because he had doubted my account of the spy, but I had to admit it was a queer story. Anyway, that didn't mean he couldn't lead the expedition well. Since Ticonderoga he had been counted on to get things done. He had lots of bouncy energy. If General Washington trusted him for the job there must be good reason.

Then I recalled that Caleb had said some of the American prisoners were going to Quebec and afterwards had clapped his mouth shut because he couldn't let out the secret. Suddenly I had a wild hope that Ben might be among them. It would be worth traveling a very hard road indeed if that were so.

As the news spread, the men's quick-tempered sourness vanished and they grew cheerful and boisterous. This meant the end of drilling and camp life. It meant action. And that was what they had enlisted for.

4

WITH ARNOLD
FOR CANADA

On the afternoon of the eleventh day since the expedition left Cambridge we reached a place on the Kennebec River known as Colburn's shipyard, a scene of great activity. Behind a row of bateaux along the bank, scores of workmen were hammering nails into unfinished boats or sealing planks with caulking knives.

Our sloop came about with a flurry of lowered sails and touched a dock. Morgan jumped ashore. We followed, springy of foot, sniffing with pleasure the fresh smell of pine shavings and glad to be rid of our cramped quarters aboard the sloop that had brought us from Newburyport. A man in a crimson coat and white breeches was striding about among the bateaux, stopping now and then to examine one and gesture to a fellow with him. Suddenly he turned and came swiftly toward us. I recognized him as Benedict Arnold.

"Glad you're here," he barked at Morgan. "We must get started."

"Are they ready?" asked Morgan, squinting at the boats.

"As ready as they'll ever be. Colonel Enos needs a few more for reserve supplies. They're not good. Green timber. Bound to leak."

At this, the one who had followed Arnold spoke up. "Colonel, I've been trying to tell you there ain't enough seasoned timber in the whole country hereabouts to build two hundred bateaux in a hurry. But hurry it was. That was my orders."

Arnold waved impatiently. "I know, Colburn. I'm not blaming you." His blue eyes were fixed on us speculatively. What he saw seemed to please him. He drew Morgan aside and began talking to him.

I examined the nearest of the boats. It was long, with pointed bow and flat stern. The ribs were of oak and the shell of overlapping pine planks. I asked a workman how much it weighed, for I had heard that we were to carry the boats around some rapids.

He studied me and my garb before replying. "Hope you've got a strong back, young fellow. You'll need it. I calc'late they weigh about four hundred pounds each."

With an effort I heaved up the bow. The boat was indeed heavy. I thought about this and what lay ahead as I rejoined the others. Some of the boatbuilders had laid down their tools and were staring at us with frank curiosity.

"You the riflemen from the West we heard about?" ventured one of them.

"And just now what is it that ye've heard about us?" piped up Jerry.

"Different things," the carpenter replied. "A man from Falmouth who was up to Cambridge said you'd steal anything not nailed down." He paused. "Said, too, you could load and fire them guns on the run and hit a plate-sized target twice as far away as a man with a musket could. Didn't know whether to believe him."

We all looked solemn, suppressing grins at the reputation that had gone ahead of us. Jerry replied that a rifle could hit a target not twice but three times as far away as a musket could.

"Like to see you do it."

"No time now," said Jerry blandly. "Lots of stuff to unload."

The carpenter's face cracked into a thin, skeptical smile. "Yeh. We had a notion it was mostly tall talk." He looked at his companions, who nodded grave agreement.

This was too much for Long Tom Jeffrey, a reckless and quarrelsome man who was one of the best shots in the company. Stepping out of the cluster of us, he drawled, "I reckon you don't know much. Want to see what a rifle can do, I'll show you."

He quickly loaded—a charge of powder from his horn into the muzzle, a small patch of greased cloth from the brass-lidded patch box in the rifle's butt, a bullet from the pouch, the cloth wrapped around the bullet, and the two vigorously tamped down the barrel with the ramrod. He glanced at the flint and cocked the piece. After a brief survey of the scene he raised the rifle to his shoulder and leveled it on a large thickset fellow wearing a broad-brimmed hat and a long cloak, who was standing about a hundred and fifty yards away talking with a man in an officer's uniform.

Tom pulled the trigger as we gazed spellbound.

Things happened fast. The large man's hat flew off. He clutched his head and whirled toward the crack of the shot. He had a brown beard. I remembered he had passed us in a canoe paddled by two Indians on the river the previous day. We had especially noted him because of the beard, for beards had long been out of fashion. The officer with him gave a roar of rage and charged toward the dock. Brownbeard picked up his hat and pounded after him. We could see the yellow band of a lieutenant colonel on the officer's sleeve.

Arnold and Morgan broke off their conference. "Who did that?" demanded Arnold. Morgan's gimlet eyes searched faces. Picking out Long Tom, he seized him by the throat and was vigorously shaking him when the officer and the bearded man of the shot-off hat arrived. The officer was furious.

"So this is what to expect from backwoods ruffians!" he spluttered. "Colonel Arnold, I protest this outrage." He glared at us. "It is too much to put up with from these—these undisciplined savages." Even in his anger he was comically like a donkey braying.

Dan Morgan was a man of justice after his own lights, but he could not abide slurs on his men. He took his hands off Tom and turned a baleful look at the officer. Before he could speak Arnold broke in. "Colonel Enos, it was a reckless, irresponsible act. Captain

Morgan will take care of the fellow. Let us not allow a foolish thing to interfere with our work. As for this gentleman, I apologize and am sorry he was startled."

His big eyes focused on Brownbeard. "Sir, I do not think I know you."

"Henry Jethro, at your service, sir," rumbled the other.

"A Massachusetts gentleman who will help me gather supplies," said Enos stiffly.

"We'll need all we can get," grunted Arnold. His stare switched to Long Tom. "What was the reason for it?" he demanded.

Tom shuffled his feet like a schoolboy hailed up before the teacher and muttered sullenly that these people had misdoubted what a rifle could do. He'd shown them.

"So you'd risk blowing a man's head off for that," snarled Arnold. "If you value your hide you'll never do the like again. And don't waste powder, d'ye hear me?"

But the boatbuilders were much impressed, admitting that no one could have done the trick with a musket. In their glum way they were amused at Enos's rage.

Something about the bearded man stirred a feeling of familiarity in the back of my mind. It was more than having seen him yesterday in the canoe; it was a vague sense of having known him somewhere before. But grope as I might for the memory, it would not come back.

We joined the sailors in unloading freight from the sloop—barrels of beef and flour, hardbread and pork;

kegs of powder; rolled sheets of lead; axes for hewing a way through the forest. When all was ashore, bateaux were dragged into the water and we began loading the stuff into them. Our company was assigned sixteen boats, four or five men to each. Two or three were to row or pole the boat in shallows. The others were to foot it along the bank and relieve the boatmen at intervals. With me were Caleb, Jerry, Solomon, and William Riddle.

Another sloop with New England troops came up and docked. Arnold, accompanied by three Indians, interrupted Morgan's supervision of the loading. "I'm going up to Gardinerstown," he said. "Join me at Fort Western tomorrow." He indicated two of the Indians. "These are my paddlers. The other is a guide. He is named Eneas. He speaks English. Remember him; he'll be carrying messages for me."

The driving force in him now released, Arnold was happy. With a gay wave of hands he sprang into a canoe and was off. Eneas and Sabatis followed in another canoe.

When we had loaded our boat the five of us sat down and idly watched as we waited for laggards to finish. The bearded man was standing apart from the crowd with his two Indians. He seemed to be giving them instructions. To emphasize a point he hunched his shoulders, thrust his head forward, and gestured with his right hand.

Suddenly, startlingly, the thing I had racked my mind for, the sense of familiarity, came to me. The hunched shoulders, the thrust of the head—these were mannerisms of the supposed sutler who had greeted two buyers of shoes in the meadow below Cambridge.

It seemed unbelievable, and for a moment I questioned it. Was my imagination running away with me? But as I considered the man's deep voice as he had spoken to Arnold and the set of his thick figure, it seemed more and more certain. The beard—had it been grown to conceal a telltale scar? But if this was the spy of Boston what was he doing here?

I spoke to Jerry. He gave the cloaked figure a long look and exclaimed, "Jemminey, I think you're right." I told the others.

"Best take it up with Morgan and Arnold," counseled Riddle.

After thinking a moment Caleb spoke. "If he's our spy he's so befooled that popinjay Enos that Arnold wouldn't believe it anyway. He didn't believe David before."

An idea came to me. It might be a bad move; on the other hand, it might scare a spy away from whatever he planned to do. I got up and walked casually toward Brownbeard, taking my time. I was within a few feet of him when he noticed me and broke off talk with the Indians. Was there a flicker of recognition in his eyes? I couldn't tell.

"Well, if it isn't Samuel Winter, the sutler!" I exclaimed.

There was no sign of shock in his face or manner. There was only an appearance of mild surprise such as anyone would have at being mistaken for another.

"Don't you remember me? I bought shoes from you less than a month ago near Cambridge."

"You have the wrong man, my friend," he replied. "I've never laid eyes on you before." Then, in that tone of false affability, "But I wish you well, sir. We all make mistakes."

The voice of Lieutenant Humphrey rang out. "Morgan's men. Those to the boats, get in and push off. The rest, start walking."

And so it ended. But not quite. In the boat I darted a glance back. Brownbeard was speaking earnestly to his Indians, whose black eyes were fixed intently upon me. One of them gripped the tomahawk at his belt. I knew then beyond all doubt that Brownbeard was indeed the dangerous man of the meadow. I would have to watch out for myself. There was no mistaking the order he had given the Indians.

Fort Western stood on the east bank of the Kennebec about eleven miles up from Colburn's shipyard. Its main structure was a big barrack built of foot-thick squared logs. This stood in a parade ground inclosed by a palisade of stout timbers. At the northeast and southwest corners of the palisade were blockhouses with projecting second stories loopholed for cannon.

The fort had been built at the start of the French and Indian War to protect Maine settlements against raids from Canada, but it was no longer garrisoned. It had been chosen as the starting point of our journey because it was at the head of navigation on the river for sailing vessels.

The rifle companies had been the first to arrive and had learned something of what it meant to carry bateaux and stores around rapids. There was a sense of

haste, for it was now September 23rd. We were racing
the approach of winter. Morgan drove us. Angered by
every difficulty, he bellowed oaths, growled orders, and
now and then pushed his massive frame against the
back of a stalled wagon.

In the midst of our labors came a scene which remained in mind because of its bearing on our later
struggle. A young lieutenant of Smith's named Steele,
accompanied by five of his men and two others who
appeared to be guides, approached Morgan.

"We are ready to leave, sir," he announced. "Our
canoes are near here. I understand I'm to have three of
your men."

Big Dan nodded. He shouted the names of those he
had selected—Jesse Wheeler, George Merchant, and
James Clifton. They came forward at once.

"You've got to travel fast," Morgan told Steele, with
emphasis. "Push up Dead River to the Height of Land
and find out what's just beyond. The Colonel is sending
a Maine man named Church to map the Carry Place,
but you'll have to go a lot further. Get back as soon as
you can. We hope to meet you at the Carry Place. Another thing, watch out for Indians. There's one up
Dead River named Natanis. Said to be in British pay.
He might take word of us to Quebec. Get him if you
can."

"Yes, sir, we'll do our best on both jobs." Steele
saluted casually and led the party away.

By noon the day after our arrival our boats and gear
had been hauled above the fort and we were tempo-
rarily free of work. I was wandering down the path

from the fort, with an eye out for small game, when, nearing yesterday's landing place, I saw two men come ashore and carry their canoe into the brush. One was a short, graceful young fellow in a fine uniform. The other was an Indian clad in shirt, breechclout, and moccasins.

The young man spoke. "Your pardon, sir. I am looking for Colonel Arnold."

"He's at the fort," I told him. On impulse I gave up thought of hunting and offered to take them to him. They might have news from the shipyard.

"Glad of your company," said the young man, smiling. "I am Aaron Burr, of Princeton in New Jersey. My friend is called Mattawock, of the Abenaki tribe hereabouts."

I told him my name. As we walked up the path I found him at no loss for words. He had much self-assurance and, at times, a sharp tongue, yet he was likable. I later learned that he was the son of the President of the College of New Jersey and, though only nineteen, had studied law.

He remarked that he was glad riflemen were leading the way rather than farmers who wouldn't know how to fend for themselves in the woods. He seemed to have a low opinion of New Englanders in general, but.he respected Arnold. Since he was on the topic, and because Enos at the shipyard and his bearded helper were much on my mind, I asked Burr's opinion of Enos.

"Pompous," he replied. "Perhaps overcautious. Puffed up by his military record. Served in the French War and the expedition to Havana in '62. Strikes me as a well-meaning dolt who shouldn't be allowed to make independent decisions."

"Who is the bearded man with him, the one helping gather supplies?"

Burr said he had seen the fellow but didn't know him. With that, he returned to his views of New Englanders. Too many of them, he said, were clodhopping bumpkins who thought themselves almighty shrewd but would believe any wild nonsense they were told.

"What sort of nonsense?" I inquired.

He grimaced. "They swap hair-raising tales of perils ahead. Wildcats as big as horses. The Dead River—frightening name, isn't it? Bottomless swamps. The Chaudière River. French for cauldron or boiler, so it swirls into caverns and scalds you to death. Faugh! Some of these witless fools are beginning to believe it impossible to reach Quebec this way. Yet my friend Mattawock knows better." He looked inquiringly at his companion.

The Indian gestured with an up-and-down waving motion. "Some true, most lies," he said. "Swamps, yes. Chaudière bad river, yes. Not easy trip. But"—and he swept his hand upward—"even Abenaki women and children make it with hunters." He glanced sidewise at the young man. "Burr not know who makes this talk." It was more a statement than a question.

"I wish I did."

The Indian was silent for several paces. When he spoke, his tone was bitter. "Chief Washington at Boston did not take help from our people. Our speakers went to him and he gave them empty words. Not trust.

Natanis could help, but Arnold thinks him spy, orders scouts to kill him."

"H-m-m. Perhaps someone muddled. Who starts this talk?"

After another thoughtful pause, Mattawock replied: "Know this, brother. There are two St. Francis people with this war party. They are for the English. They lie to your people. I have listened."

Like a flash of lightning his words brought understanding. That was Brownbeard's purpose here—to wreck, or at least delay, the expedition. I asked as casually as I could about the St. Francis people and Natanis.

The St. Francis people were a tribe of the Abenakis who had moved from southern Maine to the St. Francis River valley in Canada to escape the increasing number of settlers whose encroachments on hunting lands had thinned the game on which the Indians lived. In the last war they had sided with the French; now they were for the British as a lesser evil than the Colonials. As for Natanis, he was an Abenaki of the Kennebec who was friendly to the Maine settlers.

I scarcely noted the information, so intent was I on discovery of the false sutler's purpose, and paid small attention to Burr's remarks as we walked to the fort. There, working parties were sorting gear of New England companies which had just arrived. Arnold seemed glad to see my companion. "You've come at the right time," he exclaimed. "I need you to keep in touch with captains as they string out along the river."

Barely could I keep from blurting out charges

against the trickster who was responsible for Ben's capture and who now had ingratiated himself with the stupid Enos. But this was not the time for it. Instead, I waited until I could privately tell Morgan. He listened dubiously, but seemed interested in what I had learned about the spy's two Indians.

"You have no proof that this man is what you say," he objected. "But you were right before, so maybe the Colonel ought to hear it. Come to the Howard house tonight after supper."

In the dusk, made darker by lowering clouds, I tried to find Aaron Burr and Mattawock to confirm at least part of the story, but they had disappeared So I asked Jerry and Caleb to come along. As we started on the path to Howard's, a mile above the fort, cold rain began to fall.

We were near the place when a dog bounded to us. Following the dog were four men. We heard one say that he would be ready to leave by midafternoon. "Better make it faster, Topham," said another voice. "Arnold is in a tizzy." The speaker whistled to the dog, who trotted to his master.

"You're right, Dearborn, he's impatient," agreed a third voice.

Thus it seemed that the dog belonged to Captain Dearborn, a young New Hampshire officer who was said to be both kindly and able. We exchanged muttered greetings with the group.

The Howard home, surprisingly large, was lighted by many candles. An orderly answered our knock. Two women were clearing away supper dishes from the din-ing room as we entered. In a room on the other side of the hall were a number of officers, among them Captain Eleazar Oswald, Arnold's secretary, and Adjutant Christian Febiger, an efficient Dane, settled in Massachusetts, who was said to be good at laying out fortifications. We found Morgan chatting with Colonel Greene.

Big Dan frowned unhappily at sight of me. "I've had enough trouble with Colonel Arnold for one day. But come on, let's get it over with." He led the way to a room at the rear of the hall.

Arnold sat at a desk piled with papers. He was writing rapidly as he talked with his host, Captain Howard. "Even allowing for waste and spoilage, we should have enough rations," he was saying. "I hear it's not much over two hundred miles from here to Quebec. We can do that in four weeks at most. And Enos says we'll have forty-five days' rations."

Howard shook his head. "Quebec's less than two hundred miles from here—as a bird might fly. But you aren't birds. The rivers wind, especially Dead River. Indians are vague about distances. For them it depends on how long it takes them to make a trip, and that depends on whether they're traveling light and fast or taking their time. Your way to Quebec is a lot more than two hundred miles."

Arnold shrugged and stabbed his quill into the inkpot.

Morgan advanced into the room. Arnold was annoyed. "What is it?" he demanded.

"Something you ought to hear." Morgan's tone was

almost belligerent. "Could be serious. Go ahead, Gordon."

Arnold recognized me at once, and scowled. Nevertheless, I launched into what I had to say, which was the manner of my discovery of Brownbeard's identity. He broke harshly into the recital. "So you're at it again. Your cock-and-bull story of being captured by spies. General Gates found no evidence of it."

"But it happens to be true, Colonel," put in Caleb. "I was the one who got him out of Boston."

"Tell about the Injuns, Dave," urged Jerry hoarsely in what he thought was a whisper.

I repeated Mattawock's information about the two Indians with the bearded man and the tales they were telling, adding that Burr knew about it.

At this, Arnold seemed faintly interested. He stared at me thoughtfully for a moment, then shook his head. "It doesn't wash. Colonel Enos knows this fellow and trusts him."

Caleb spoke again. "Sir, there's no trusting anybody these times. Could be Colonel Enos was taken in by a slick talker."

Arnold threw up his hands impatiently. "All right, I'll have the messenger Eneas look into it when he goes down there."

Abruptly he returned to his writing, dismissing the lot of us. His mind was back on the business of getting to Quebec.

Big Dan went with us to the door of the house. He was angry but keeping it in. "Get sleep," he growled. "We leave tomorrow."

As the door closed Jerry whispered, "Go on. I'll catch up." When he rejoined us he was lugging a roasted chicken. He explained that he had seen it on a table by a window of the kitchen as we went to talk to Arnold. "Reckoned maybe I could open the window from outside, and I was right," he said smugly. He snorted at my halfhearted suggestion that he take it back.

"Are ye daft, Dave? We've got to eat well while we can."

5

RUSHING RIVER

The first two days of travel above Fort Western were not bad, though at times it was hard to keep the clumsy boat from swinging broadside to the current and tipping over. Ticonic Falls, some eighteen miles beyond the fort, was the first real obstacle. The carry around it was only about 200 yards but it took several hours, what with unloading the boats, taking up the barrels and kegs—four men with crossed poles to each—going back to muscle up the boats, and then reloading.

Above this place the Kennebec began to show us what it could do. There was a stretch called the Five-mile Riffle where water churned around rocks and over shallows and we had to wade hip-deep in the cold flood, dragging the boats by ropes. Sometimes a man stepped into a hole and disappeared, coming up puffing and swearing. The bateaux sprang leaks. Often, despite our best efforts, a boat slammed against rocks. With each slam a new leak opened.

In the beginning everybody took the mishaps easily.

There were jokes about ways to keep the boats afloat—such as boring holes in the bottom to let the water run out. But gradually humor wore thin. Crews fell to cursing the boatbuilders and whoever had persuaded Arnold to use bateaux on this devil of a river.

We were near the end of the rapids when a thing happened that won me a friend and later made the difference between life and death for me. The boat ahead was in trouble, lashing from side to side in the tumbling current. Suddenly a canoe, headed downstream and steered by an Indian, shot around a bend. The bateau swerved wildly into the canoe's path. The Indian sprang up, made a desperate sweep with his paddle, and raced past with feet to spare. But his new course took him into a perilous, rock-strewn millrace near the opposite bank.

He skillfully avoided danger until he was abreast of us, where a cross current swept his frail craft against a boulder. The shock pitched him off balance and out of the canoe. Catlike, he stretched his arms before him to break the fall, but his hands must have slipped on the wet rock, for his head struck it and he slithered into the churning water. When he came up he wasn't swimming, though the current washed him bobbingly on.

Yelling to the others to beach the boat, I jumped in and, striking out, soon caught up with the Indian. Somehow I got him ashore. After my breath was back I looked him over and was surprised to see that he was just a boy, probably not more than fifteen. His brown face was clean-lined and good-looking. Carefully I ex-

amined his head. As I could feel no cracked bones, I decided he was only stunned.

Jerry and Caleb came down the bank, Jerry berating me for foolhardiness. We lugged the boy back to the boat and were about to put him aboard when he came to, eyes open but glassy. We laid him on the pebbles and after a moment he sat up, bracing himself with stiff arms. He began to speak in a soft, strange tongue.

Seeing our puzzlement, he stopped, took a deep breath, and seemed to collect his wits. He spoke again, this time in slow, careful English. His eyes went from one to another of us. "Who pull me out?" he asked.

"He did," replied Jerry, jerking his thumb toward me. "And 'twas lucky for you. You would have been drowned."

The Indian regarded me a moment, then asked my name. When I told him he repeated it in his soft, slurred English. "Me, Muskosis, Beaver, Kennebec, Abenaki," he announced, in the Indian way of giving first the personal name, then the clan, the subtribe, and the big tribe or nation. "A man of your people taught me English at Swan Island," he said with pride. He got to his feet and stood, swaying slightly. Then to me: "You my brother."

There were stories of Indian gratitude to white men, but such was our mistrust of our savage foes in the West that I had only half believed them. Now it came to me that there might be an Indian side to the argument. So I said quickly: "And you are *my* brother."

The boy rubbed his head. I could see him stiffen against a wince that would not have become a warrior. "Muskosis," he repeated. "But to English I am Mike," he added gravely. "That is my name in English— Mike."

It struck us as funny, but we suppressed our grins. "And a very good name it is, that," said Jerry.

After we had built a fire and dried out a bit we crossed in the bateau and looked at the canoe. There was a big hole in one side and the paddle was missing, but the frame seemed undamaged. We learned that Mike was on his way to meet his uncle, who was none other than Burr's companion, Mattawock.

At this I suggested that he forget the canoe and join us until Mattawock caught up with the expedition. But he refused. It would be easy to patch the canoe with birch bark, using small cedar roots as thread, and to whittle a paddle. What matter if it took longer to make pitch to seal the patch? We offered him some pitch from the small store we carried, and also a bit of bread and beef, which he gravely accepted.

A number of boats had passed us since the mishap, and now we set off to make up for lost time. At our last sight of the Indian boy he was standing by the canoe, arm upraised in farewell.

As I look back on what we endured on the way to Quebec I think that often we did not realize the extent of our trials. This is not to say we weren't painfully aware of them at the worst moments, but once they were over and we'd had a few hours of rest we could wipe out the memory of them and, with new spirit, start afresh. It may have been partly our state of mind; we were centered on getting there. Or it may be that under such conditions nature mercifully pulls a veil over the immediate past. At any rate, I marvel we managed the thing at all.

On the day after meeting the Indian boy we came to a whirlpool at a bend of the river and beyond that a stretch of white water leading to Skowhegan Falls. Here the carry was up the steep face of a rock about 35 feet high, with a cleft in the center. For generations Indians had been pulling their canoes up the rock without great difficulty, but with the big 400-pound boats it was quite another matter.

Somehow it was done. Tugging, pushing, straining, crushed against the sides of the cleft, feet slipping, using our last reserve of strength, we slowly got the boats to the top. During the next two days we made twelve miles against the swift water. We reached Norridge-wock Falls and camped below the torrent. The next morning we spent patching the boats. Afterward, there was a mile-long, uphill carry.

It was nearing twilight when we dropped on a flat expanse of rock above the falls. Some hunched wearily, hands around knees, others lay on their backs. We had made it. And blast Dan Morgan and his yelling.

I looked around at the intermingled riflemen of the three companies. Some yards away a big, husky woman was sewing up a rent in a man's shirt, whose owner watched approvingly, his torso bare to the cold wind. The woman was Mrs. Grier and the man was her husband, a sergeant in Hendricks' company. She was going with her man wherever he went. She was a good woman and highly respected. Seeing her now from the depths of fatigue, I wondered at her fortitude.

There was a stir among the men as Arnold emerged from the path through the woods with Morgan behind him. The contrast between them was striking. Arnold was spick and span. Morgan had reverted to his woods garb of breechclout, leggings, and tattered wool shirt, and on his face was a stubble of beard. He was driving and helping us to heroic efforts and he looked it.

Early in the morning we pushed off, heading into the unknown, for here we left behind the last houses along the Kennebec. For two days, however, the going was easy and pleasant. The river, bestrewn with grassy islands, was comparatively calm and was filled with trout we caught by the hundreds. Back of the river's steep banks was an open forest of beech, elm, and birch, with some spruce and pine. The hardwoods, already casting their leaves, were brilliant with colors. The men who walked found easy footing. Spirits rose; it was not such a bad life after all.

But on the third day, after passing Devil's Falls, things changed. The river became shallow and boulder-strewn. The country was gloomy, forbidding, with mountains closing in on both sides of the stream. From low gray clouds came bursts of cold rain. When at times the mist lifted we saw snow on the uplands. On the afternoon of the fifth day above Norridgewock a mountain shaped like a sugarloaf was sighted. It was the landmark to the Great Carry Place to Dead River. Above this point the Kennebec was impassable for bateaux.

We landed on a grassy bank and unloaded. A few crews who had tents pitched them. The rest made lean-tos of poles covered with spruce branches and floored with springy spruce beds. That night the cloud mass that had pelted us with showers dropped on us a cold steady downpour. At dawn, as the rain continued, Morgan passed the word to take the day for rest. The first of Greene's bedraggled division began coming up, lining the shore with their boats. Most of the riflemen huddled under their shelters and slept, saving their strength for what lay ahead.

What lay ahead, we soon discovered, was back-breaking toil. During the night the rain stopped, the sky cleared, and by daylight the temperature was near freezing.

After breakfast Morgan appeared with a stranger, a tall, solemn man, the Lieutenant Church who had been sent to map this place. We clustered around the two as Church began talking.

"It's about twelve to thirteen miles to Dead River," he said, pointing with a stick toward the west. With the stick he drew a sort of map on the wet ground. "The river comes down from the northwest, like this," he said. "You'll hit it at a bend where it turns north, then east, until it joins the Kennebec about ten miles above here.

"There's three ponds between here and the river," he continued. "Call it three and a half miles to the first one. Rough going around ridges. Have to chop a path for the boats. Say three-quarters to the next one—what you might call a stale pond. Past that, a good mile and a half to the third, a big one. Then three miles to a creek running into the river. The first two pretty hard— up over a ridge—and the last through a bad bog. I blazed a trail."

He dropped his stick. "Any questions?" he asked.

There were. He answered them all, clearly and methodically.

As Morgan called the company together Jerry muttered: " 'Tis like what the horse said to himself after fallin' into a swamp, 'Me hide is in for a rough curryin'!' This man Church is not one to overstate the case, you might say."

And so it proved. There were axes for thirty-eight riflemen, and they began to clear a path. The rest of us loaded ourselves with stores slung on carry poles. The three and a half miles to the first pond seemed like thirty and the "ridges" were mountains. Like human pack horses we strained, slipped, slid, and sometimes fell flat. Jeers and laughter were the lot of those who took tumbles and of any awkward axman who laid a tree wrong. When we got to the pond, which was actually a small lake, we took a rest and enjoyed the arrival of the mud-spattered Pennsylvanians, exchanging pleasant insults with them. On our way back we met the first of Greene's men.

There is little to be told of the next three days, as we went back and forth to the steady *chock-chock* of axes. We got the rest of the stores and then our boats to the first pond, over it, and on to the second. We were well fed, for the first pond seethed with trout caught as fast as you could bait a hook.

The second pond was different, deserving of Church's description "stale." It was surrounded by a bog studded with the skeletons of dead trees, the water near shore was covered with yellow slime, and over it all hung an odor of rot. We completed our final carry to this place late in the afternoon and were slumped beside our boats when Jerry suddenly sprang to his feet and pointed at a canoe. "That's queer," he observed. "We're the first here, yet it's coming from the other direction."

We hallooed to the strangers and squished through the bog to meet them. Three people got out of the boat with the careful motions of men who have been sick or have driven themselves to the limit of endurance.

Morgan greeted the first of the three. "Steele!" he exclaimed.

The man's smile was a grimace. He was thinned to whipcord and his eyes were bloodshot from exhaustion and lack of sleep. "Right glad to see you, Captain," he croaked. "Had to leave the rest of the party behind fixing a canoe. After I report to Colonel Arnold I'll go back with grub for them."

Morgan bellowed for somebody to start a fire and cook trout. "Arnold ought to be here tomorrow," he told Steele. "You stay here and eat. What did you find?"

The scout's story was disappointing. The distance had been misjudged. Maybe it was forty miles from here to Canada the way a goose flies but by twisting Dead River it was twice that. On the river it would be easy for a time, but then came more riffles and a chain of ponds between mountains toward the source, with tough spots between them.

"What about the Height of Land?"

"With light loads and full bellies, it wouldn't be bad. From the last pond you take off up and over some ridges by an Indian path. But short of grub, it's another thing. We got to a creek that runs down into Chaudière Lake, or Meguntic as some calls it. At least it seemed to. I climbed a tree to see its course. Country looks swampy. We couldn't stay because we were almost out of vittles. No game there. If we hadn't got two moose back on Dead River we'd have starved."

Morgan rubbed his chin thoughtfully. "Can you draw Arnold a map?"

"Have one already."

From his haversack Steele produced a piece of birch bark. On it was scratched a wriggling line that he said was Dead River, then dots for ponds, and a wavery line representing the Height of Land. Beyond the Height marks indicated a way around Chaudière Lake and on to the St. Lawrence by way of the Chaudière River.

"Found this in a cleft stick near the cabin of that Indian Natanis, the one the Colonel wanted us to get. He wasn't around but signs showed he'd been there a day or two before. Reckon he left this to guide somebody to Quebec. Indians most likely."

Morgan's grunt meant nothing one way or another. Remembering Mattawock's insistence that Natanis was friendly, I wondered how he had known to avoid the scouts and why, after that, he had left the map where it could easily be found. It was a puzzling thing.

Most of the next day we spent helping the choppers complete a path to the third pond, using axes Arnold had taken from the musket companies. From this lake we could see the snow-covered crest of the massive Dead River Mountain. It was a cheering token that we were near the end of the carry. But it was here that the sickness began. Some men were racked by rheumatism because of toil and exposure. Many had stomach pains and vomiting. We were a worn, ill-tempered lot when we began the last portage.

It was up and down, and a bateau was an almost intolerable burden for four men. On the up slopes its weight fell upon those behind and on down slopes upon those carrying the bow. We were thankful when the ridges ended and we saw before us what seemed to be a level meadow.

But this was the worst of all. Like many such deceptive places in the north woods, the matted grass grew out of a quagmire and would not bear a man's weight. In the muck beneath, and preserved by it, were dead spruces with hard, pointed branches like sharp stakes. As we sank to the knees in the stuff our feet and legs were cruelly slashed. With wild oaths and howls of pain the bearers lurched forward a step at a time. Toward dusk we came to the creek leading to Dead River and dropped the boats on firm ground. We looked at each other glumly, mud-plastered, foul-smelling creatures.

As we washed ourselves in the icy water of the creek a white man and two Indians with a canoe came slogging through the mire. The white man told us that he was going to Sartignan in Canada to sound out the inhabitants and arrange to buy supplies. He gestured toward the Indians. "They're carrying letters from Arnold to friends in Canada."

One of the Indians was Eneas.

When the three launched their canoe and started down the creek Solomon stared after them, frowning. "No sense to it," he growled. "Sending word of us to Quebec."

Caleb told him that Arnold knew people there from his trading days.

"But he's trusting Injuns," objected Solomon stubbornly.

At the time I thought little of it, considering Solomon prejudiced against all Indians. But later we were to remember his words.

Major Meigs' men arrived the next day. Enos was still behind. We returned to the third pond and brought the rest of the stores. Before dark we launched our boats and rowed for an hour up the delightfully placid river before making camp.

It had taken us a week, but we had passed the Great Carrying Place. And we devoutly hoped we would never have to pass it again.

6

PERIL IN THE WILDERNESS

It was hard to believe. Surely there should be game in these parts. But so far I had seen nothing. This morning, after a day of good progress on Dead River, Morgan had decided on a hunt, hoping for rabbits and squirrels to make restoring broths for the sick, and a deer or moose for the rest of us. Yet it seemed that Lieutenant Steele was right; animals, large or small, were exceedingly scarce in this land.

There had been a few shots, though there was no way to tell whether they had been fired in earnest or by those few among us who, against orders, would pull a trigger for the fun of it once they were out of Morgan's sight. It seemed better to go farther from the river, so for a time I stalked through the woods until, coming to a likely spot, I leaned watchfully against a tree. Soon I saw a slight movement in a spruce thicket about fifty yards away. I crouched, reckoning it might be a deer. Barely had I dropped to my hunkers when I heard a shot and the thwack of a bullet into the tree bark where an instant before my shoulders had been. I slumped to the ground, rifle ready, thinking fast.

Had some fool mistaken me for a deer? Not likely. Besides, the sound had not been the crack of a rifle but the duller report of a musket. Who would be using a musket here? One of the scare stories had been that Canadian Indians were laying in wait for us. Was this an ambush of the company or was someone after me alone? Tensely I lay, watchful, playing dead. Moments passed. At last a branch stirred in the thicket. There was another short wait, then an Indian cautiously came out, musket in hand.

My rifle came instantly to my shoulder and the sights made a straight line to him. "Drop that gun," I yelled.

He leaped sidewise like a wildcat, bounding for the nearest tree, and I fired. But he had been too fast for me. I sprang up, sheltering behind my tree trunk, and began to load. As I poured the powder down the barrel I heard a footstep behind me. Whirling, I met the shock of a hurtling body that drove me to the ground. In that split second of collision I saw an Indian with a knife in his hand. Then we were locked in struggle, with me desperately clutching the Indian's wrist as he tried to push the knife into my throat.

He was strong, sinewy, and slippery as a fish. I couldn't twist the knife out of his hand and was too occupied to get at my own knife. I butted my head into his fiercely painted face. He merely grunted. I grabbed his throat with my free hand. He tore loose. I tried to roll him off, tried to get a thumb in an eye, tried to knee him, tried every fighting trick I knew. But he clung tenaciously, and in the trial of muscles the point of the knife pressed closer.

Looking back on it, I don't know how long the struggle lasted. It must have been fairly brief, though it seemed an eternity. It ended with the sound of a blow. The Indian twitched, his arms slowly relaxed, and the knife dropped from his hand.

Weak and giddy, I slid from beneath the inert body that a moment before had been so ferociously alive. I got to my knees, to my feet. Facing me was a young Indian with a bloody tomahawk in his hand. I stared at him in amazement. "Mike!" I croaked.

"Hurt?"

"No. But if you hadn't come when you did—"

"I follow him but maybe stay too far behind," said Muskosis in a tone of triumph tinged with a little self-criticism. He turned the Indian over. "Look," he directed. "You know?"

It was only then that I recognized my would-be murderer beneath his paint as one of Brownbeard's two henchmen. I vividly recalled the scene at the shipyard —the spy pointing me out to the Indians as I left in the boat. I felt a little sick.

"You saved my life," I mumbled.

"My brother save me in the white water," Mike gravely replied.

I rested my hand on the boy's shoulder, lacking words to say what I felt. Picking up my rifle, I finished loading it and looked toward the tree where the other Indian had hidden.

"He gone now, I think," said Mike. "When he see Natanis after him he run."

Natanis again. I asked Mike what he had to do with Natanis—and why he himself was here.

He stared at the ground for a moment, then suddenly fixed blank eyes on me. "Indian understand, but you—maybe not." He went on to speak rapidly of guidance from the Beaver spirit and of advice from a medicine man who could foresee the future. "He tell me to be here now," he said. It was a roundabout Indian approach. And never have I been able to decide how much Indians really believe in such stuff and how much is just a form of speech.

"My brother does not tell me what is in his heart," I said, trying to speak like an Indian orator.

Muskosis thought that over a moment, nodded, and launched into a fairly simple account. When his uncle, Mattawock, had learned of Arnold's intentions toward Natanis, he had sent Mike to warn his friend. Mike had found Natanis shortly before the scouts had arrived. The Indian's feelings had been hurt by the Americans' suspicion of him but had decided the mistake could be cleared up later. He had left the scouts the map and had watched them from a safe distance. Mike had set out to rejoin his uncle. It was on the return trip that he had had the accident and we had met.

"Why did you come back again?"

"The two with the hairy one were of St. Francis. Mattawock know those three make trouble. When they left Enos and went into the woods he sent me to trail them. He not leave Burr."

Mattawock couldn't figure what they were up to— maybe to warn the English at Quebec, maybe to kill Natanis or me. They had carried a canoe and so had Mike. A half-day above Enos's camp they had taken to the river. So had Mike. They had traveled fast, slipping by the expedition at night. They had passed our company a night's camp below the Great Carry Place.

The trail had led up Dead River. Near Natanis's camp, not far from here, Mike had heard his friend's crow call and had joined him. They had watched the search for Natanis by Brownbeard and his Indians, who had spent most of yesterday at it. During the night the white man had unaccountably disappeared. Perhaps he had left for Quebec. The Indians came back to this place, spying on Morgan's movements. Quite evidently they had had me in mind.

"The one who got away now follows Brownbeard, I guess."

"I go after him with Natanis, quick. We take canoe hidden up river."

"Good luck. Be careful. Maybe we'll meet ahead."

Mike regarded me thoughtfully. "Keep secret?" he asked.

"For you, of course."

"Some of our people watch this war party. They go to Meguntic. Might be trouble there. Bad country. They help if can. But you not tell Arnold this. No good—yet."

I promised that my mouth would be closed. We shook hands. Mike turned and vanished swiftly into the woods.

When at last the hunters had gathered by the river bank I told my teammates of the ambush and how Mike had saved me. They were much concerned, and loud in praise of the Indian boy.

"That clinches it," muttered Jerry. "Benedict Arnold is a fool. He'd best have listened to ye at first."

The hunting had been poor. Morgan was in a bad mood. We made a lot of mileage that afternoon, turning and twisting with the stream, and always with the great cluster of snow-covered peaks called Dead River Mountain seeming to march along with us to the south.

Those who had some knowledge of this north country said they had never seen at this season such weather as soon struck us. The rain began gently but grew ever harder as a rising wind lashed the forest. The boats had to be dragged by ropes through the raging shallows.

For hours the fury grew, the wind mounting to a steady roar, the rain driving slantwise in sheets. Trees toppled around us. The air was oddly warm. At long last the rain ended, but the floods didn't.

Our next mishap was little short of a disaster. We came to a rapid where the current was so wild that before we could drag all boats ashore two capsized and broke up on rocks. All provisions in them were lost, along with some rifles.

That night Benedict Arnold called a council of war.

Jerry and I crept through the underbrush until we were within earshot of the figures around the fire. Arnold was calm but seemed less confident than usual.

"I want your opinions," he began. "We have lost a lot of food. What's left is not enough to get us to the French settlements. I'm taking steps to speed up Colonel Enos but I don't know how much food he has. We ought to be able to live off the land for a little while. But we have sick who should be sent back. Without them, I think the rest can get through. I propose to push ahead of you to Sartignan to buy provisions and get them to you on the Chaudière."

His glance circled the ring of officers. "It's a gamble. General Washington expects us to get there. The alternative is to give up our hopes and scurry back fast. What are your views?"

Morgan was a thing to see in the flickering firelight, wild-haired, bearded, and somehow tremendous. "Go on," he growled. "Too late to turn back. We'll make out on nothing, if need be."

"Major Meigs?"

Return J. Meigs, a Connecticuter who was called "Back-up" because of his peculiar first name, grinned. "We'll boil our moccasins. I've heard of such."

"Captain Dearborn?"

The officer was stroking the black dog at his feet, the one I remembered from Fort Western. Dearborn seemed thin and wasted. "I concur," he said. "We can do it. We *must*." Captain Oswald approved. One by one, the other officers agreed.

Arnold smiled. He turned to Captain Hanchet, who had an underslung jaw that made him look determined. "Take fifty picked men and follow me. Cut a path over the Height of Land. Then go to the Chaudière and see the provender I send back gets to the rest."

The sick men—a surprising number from the companies gathered here—were picked out the next morning. It was understood that Enos would provide for them and the feeble of Greene's companies so they could reach the Maine settlements. Enos was then to come up with fifteen days' rations for us and bring as many of his own men as he could thus supply.

Arnold, Steele, Church, and a few others set out on their mission. Hanchet's group followed. That evening the wind swung to the north, cold, keen, piercing. Sleet began to fall. It soon turned to snow, which came down all night.

We reached the chain of ponds toward the headquarters of the river. These small lakes lay between mountain ridges in wild, gloomy, tumbled country. They were connected by brooks, mostly small and hard to find. Here we finished the last of the pork. The remaining flour was doled out little by little. When fires were possible we baked it, Indian fashion, in hot ashes. But often it was stirred in water to make a tasteless paste called "bleary."

The chain of ponds we battled for two days. On the morning of the third we came to a large pond lying beneath two mountains. It was the last of the chain. We crossed it and landed on the north side where a great granite cliff, an outpost of the Height of Land, brooded down upon us. It was snowing again.

We were taking a short rest when a canoe paddled by a white man and an Indian came up the pond. The white man was one of Arnold's messengers.

"Bad news, Captain," he announced abruptly. "Colonel Enos"—and he spat in the snow as if to cleanse his mouth of the name—"isn't bringing you vittles. His division turned back two days ago." He went on to say that Greene had delivered the sick men and had repeated Arnold's orders to bring on fifteen days' rations. There had been a council. Despite Greene's and Major Bigelow's arguments, Enos's division had decided to quit.

"Why, the white-livered—" began Solomon. A storm of incredulous, growled curses arose from the crowd.

"Enos himself voted to go on, but his captains overruled him," continued the messenger. "Said we'd never make Quebec. And Enos was mighty easy persuaded. Those people have turned plumb chicken-hearted."

Long afterwards I learned that Enos had been court-martialed on his return but had been acquitted. He had claimed a mix-up of orders and said that Arnold had overestimated the supplies he had, or some such thing. But I still think it was a craven act, with a spy at the bottom of it.

Big Dan glared ferociously at the messenger. "This means we'll have to go maybe a hundred miles to the settlements on what little we've got. And it means what started out as eleven hundred men is down to about six hundred fifty, what with the drop-outs, the sick, and now this bunch."

The man nodded agreement. "Greene got only two barrels of flour out of Enos. I'm going to catch up with the Colonel." With that, he and the Indian shouldered their canoe and trudged north.

A new surge of curses burst from the men. They hoped Enos and his companies would die on the way.

"That help's your feelings but not much else," broke in Morgan harshly. "H'ist them boats and get on the trail."

"You mean carry these things over a mountain?" blurted an unbelieving voice.

"It's not a mountain. It's a rise over a ridge."

"But the rest are leaving most of theirs. Arnold told the New Englanders to take only one boat a company."

"Pay no mind to that. We've seven boats left and we need 'em to carry ammunition down the Chaudière. This is the easiest way, once we're over the hump. Drag 'em, if you have to."

For a moment it was touch and go, as Morgan eyed the sullen, mutinous faces around him. Suddenly a sardonic look came over his big, craggy face and he changed his tune. "It's said to be just four and a half miles to a stream. We can go by water then." He paused, looking at us with gimlet eyes. "Are you men?" he asked plaintively, "or babies?" Another pause. "Can you do it or not?"

It was an adroit appeal to pride—to our fierce pride in ourselves—and I knew he had us. There was a half minute of silence—of black looks at Morgan. Then Long Tom Jeffries growled, "You know we're men." Another voice sighed resignedly, "All right, let's go."

So began, in midmorning of a dreary snow-filled day, what lived ever afterward, in the memories of the weary, half-starved men who endured it, as the Terrible Carry.

For a while the way led up gently. The ground was swampy and strewn with wind-felled trees, rotting logs, and all manner of obstacles that Hanchet's men had barely dented. After a long time we came to a steeper climb where the jumble was even worse and the struggle up the slope was almost beyond bearing. Amid rocks and logs, through pitfalls hidden by snow and forest debris, we lugged the freight and carried or dragged the boats. We twisted ankles, fell, lay exhausted. Our shoulders were raw and bloody.

Three hours or more after leaving the pond we came to the end of the climb. Here, with greater heights on either side, the trees were stunted and wind-whipped. It seemed to my dizzied senses a nightmare place, beyond the ordinary world.

We made a change of course to the west and stumbled down through the bleak afternoon of whirling snowflakes. Mechanically we went on and on, driven by a half-crazy determination. At last we reached a flat, open space where the footing was firm. We staggered across it until we came to a small, snow-shrouded creek.

"This is it, boys," honked Daniel Morgan. "Called the Beautiful Meadow. And this is the stream that goes down to Chaudière. You've done well."

Numbly we dropped our burdens. Whatever the name of this place, it seemed 'beautiful to us now. In the gloom of the early northern dusk we collected branches from the nearby woods for fires, cooked and ate an ashcake apiece, and rolled ourselves in our blankets. We are in Canada at last, I thought, and fell instantly asleep.

7

TIME OF STARVING

The sky had cleared during the night and the air was bitter cold. The snow-covered meadow lay glittering under the morning sun. This open space was long, narrow, and parklike, studded here and there with a few majestic elms whose bare branches formed graceful designs. On either side dark groves of evergreens were interspersed among forests of birches. Behind us woods covered the slopes of the Height of Land. Ahead, a considerable hill, steep-sided and round-topped, stood alone. To the west were blue mountain heights.

After the tangled country we had left, the place was indeed pleasant. It seemed a good omen, a promise that our hardships were nearly over. Yet here began troubles and ill luck worse than any we had hitherto survived.

The Pennsylvanians who had followed us were camped nearby. During the morning the companies of Dearborn and Goodrich joined us. Big Dan had set off early to have a look at the country toward the lake.

Dearborn, accompanied by his dog, came asking for Morgan. His face was thin and feverish. Lieutenant Humphrey told him of Morgan's lone scouting trip.

"Captain Goodrich and I are going to push our companies on," said Dearborn. "We want to be well down the lake by dark, if possible. We have two boats and a canoe. Captain Ward will follow as soon as his company gets here."

Humphrey looked doubtful. "When Steele came back from this place he said the stretch ahead looked swampy. Captain Morgan wanted to see. Better wait for his report."

Dearborn replied that with rations so low, they had to keep going. So, after getting their boats in the creek, Goodrich set off down the bank with his company and Dearborn followed in his canoe, his men tramping after him. Soon all of them disappeared into the woods to the north. The Pennsylvanians left next. Hendricks and Smith didn't like the route the others had taken but Smith, a stubborn man, was sure they could reach the lake by taking a course more to the northeast. By mid-afternoon the remaining companies of our little army, under Colonel Greene and Major Bigelow, had arrived.

Some time later a stranger in a small canoe came paddling up the creek, landed, and banked his craft. He was another of Arnold's messengers, a Maine man whose gray eyes appraised us shrewdly. Questioned about the men in the woods, he said he had passed a bateau on the lake but had seen nothing of any marchers. Scanning our boats, he remarked that it must have been pretty hard getting them over the hill, meaning the Height of Land.

One of our lads named Charlie Jacobs, feeling rested and perky, drawled: " 'Twarn't much. All in knowin' how. We got into 'em and poled 'em up the hill, then we just let go and slid the rest of the way." This drew appreciative grins. Another picked up the japery. "And how we whizzed down!" he marveled. "Times were, I thought we'd took wing."

"Mighty funny," commented the messenger, wooden-faced. "I don't want to down your high spirits, but once you're past the lake a bateau may be more trouble than help. The Chaudière River, what I've seen of it, is devilish. Risky even for canoes."

He told us that Arnold had started down the lake early this morning after spending the night in a bark hut halfway to the foot. "He sent me back to warn you people who haven't got boats to stay out of the country between here and the lake. It's bad. Thing to do is keep to high ground east of here for a time, then turn north to the foot of the lake and the river."

Humphrey agreed vigorously.

"There's other news," continued the stranger. "The fellow who went to Canada with those two Indians is back from Sartignan. Met Arnold on the lake. Says the Frenchies are collecting vittles for you."

We whooped with joy.

Near dusk Big Dan came shambling back. His leggings and scarred thighs were coated with muck. As he squatted before a fire thawing out, Humphrey told him of Arnold's messages and of the companies which had gone ahead. "Dearborn said he had a map showing a path to the lake," he explained. "He was in a hurry, and that pigheaded Smith wouldn't listen to caution."

Morgan jumped to his feet. "Smith and Hendricks had no business leaving without my order," he roared. "The others ought to have known better. They're in trouble. Down toward the lake is no place for people to go afoot. We're going only because we've got boats." When he simmered down he described what he had learned. It amounted to this.

The lower reach of the stream ran through country that seemed all right at first but turned into a big elder and cedar swamp, knee-to-waist-deep, ice-coated, and crossed by confusing sloughs too deep to ford. Dearborn's map was a copy of one made years ago by a British officer who had come through this area. Maybe the Redcoat had had a dry season, or things had changed since then. But there was no trail to the lake; he had spent a long time casting about for one. The map to trust was the Indian one Steele had brought back. Greene had a copy of it and a guide who thought he knew the way, but the trail might be hard to follow.

He outlined his plan for us. In the morning we would launch the boats, two men to a boat until the channel deepened. The rest would follow the creek a mile or so, then get aboard and go to the lake. On the way, we might find traces of the ones in the swamp. With that, he walked over to talk to Greene.

At dawn we began our job while Greene's men shouldered their packs and trudged off to the right, keeping to high ground. The stream turned and twisted like the track of a crazy snake but we went down it joking and singing as if we hadn't a care in the world. Listening to the cheerful uproar, I was proud of the company. There were a lot of good fellows in it and some mean ones, but good or bad, they were tough as horsehide and springy as spruce boughs and in a tight spot you could count on all of them.

We hallooed from our overladen boats into the tangle on either side, but we got no answer nor did we see any sign of those who had come this way. We reached the lake and rowed up its eastern shore beside a bog. Here we met Dearborn and one of his men in the canoe. They had spent the night at the bark hut. Now they were going back to look for the missing companies. We rowed on, past rising wooded ground, until we came to the hut. Then we made fires and wolfed another ashcake apiece.

Morgan was worried. His urge for speed and his anxiety about the lost companies were at war within him. He sent Sergeant Porterfield and Tom Chapman back to inspect the shore along the bog. The sky was beginning to thicken. More snow was on the way.

Porterfield and Chapman returned several hours later. With them were two shivering, mud-plastered men of Goodrich's company. Dearborn had found them beside a deep slough. Porterfield said two fellows in the bateau of Smith's company were also searching the waterways.

The rescued ones could tell us little. The companies had struggled through the morass the previous afternoon, gradually dispersing and getting nowhere. These two had spent the night on a hummock, and the morning wading through mud and water to a slough they couldn't cross. But they thought that with the aid of two bateaux and the canoe most of the men would make it through, if they could be located. They remarked on a strange thing. They had seen some Indians pulling exhausted men out of the mire. Didn't know who they were but they seemed friendly.

At this, it was hard to keep silent. It meant that Muskosis had spoken truly. The Abenakis were helping.

Morgan brooded over the news briefly, then made his decision. We started for the lower end of the lake. The river that was the lake's outlet was sighted as night closed on us. We made camp. Morgan swore that tomorrow we were going places fast.

And that was what we did—for a time at least. The messenger had been right. The Chaudière—"The Cauldron"—was dangerous. It descended in an almost unbroken series of rapids, foaming over ledges, racing continually between the steep banks of its crooked course.

The speed was exhilarating but the work was hard on men who for so long had eaten so little. Steersmen labored frantically; oarsmen tugged and threshed to help them; men in the bows jabbed at rocks with poles to fend off destruction. On this wild river there was no relief from effort or concentration; we were keyed constantly to peril and split-second action.

After quite a while of this we rounded a bend and shot into a rapid steeper than any we had seen. Our boat was following Morgan's when the other suddenly tilted as it swept over a fall. I glimpsed men rising, grabbing rifles. Then our boat took the plunge. It hit a ledge with a grinding crash and crumbled.

Half strangled, I was swept like a leaf by the torrent. Heads bobbed up around me. The current bore us to shore. We reached an eddy in a bend of the river and were able to crawl out. Morgan whirled around, eying the scene. Two boats had disappeared. Wrecks of the others were on or near the bank on our side of the river, for which the set of the current at this point was responsible.

Big Dan shouted: "Hullo, boys, gather here."

It was bad but it was not utter ruin. After we started a fire a tally showed all present save one poor fellow from Morgan's boat. Most rifles had been saved because many had kept them strapped to their backs. We had the powder and ball each carried. We went to the wrecks we could reach and salvaged sodden blankets and some kegs of powder and ball. But not a trace of flour remained.

As we dried ourselves and the blankets around fires we considered our plight. We believed we had come down the river about fifteen miles. It was estimated to be nearly seventy miles from the lake, by the river, to Sartignan. Still fifty-five to go. It was a long way for people without food.

Around noon groups from the lost companies began to arrive, after some quite remarkable marching once they were free of the swamps. They streamed in, gaunt, tattered fellows of various commands. Among them was Dr. Senter, a dignified young man whose medicine chest had been lost in the wrecking of our boats.

In no sort of order we set off, all driven by the conviction that we had to walk as long as there was light.

The events of the next two days remain for the most part a blur in my memory, a half-sensed time of slogging up and down hills, of clawing through spruce thickets, of forcing step after step along the never-ending way above the tumbling river. Hunger was no longer a thing that gnawed at the stomach; it had become a dangerous weakness of the body. A few incidents, however, stand out like objects suddenly come upon in a fog.

One of these was the sight of men devouring joints of raw, bloody meat. Beside them on the snow lay a furry black pelt. After studying it I realized it was the skin of Dearborn's faithful dog. The sight made me sick and angry. Later, we passed Dearborn, propped against a tree, resting. His deep-set eyes were anguished. Starving men had demanded his dog and he had given it to them, sorry both for the dog and them.

Still later we came upon three Indians squatting around a fire. Some militiamen lay beside them. The Indians were cooking something in a pot. One of them got up and trotted toward me. "Dave!" he exclaimed.

Dully I gripped Mike's hand. "How goes it?" I asked. Mike clasped his lean stomach. "Bad hunting." He pointed to the militiamen. "Sick. We bring in canoe. Make broth." He beckoned me to a canoe drawn up on the bank. From it he produced the body of a raccoon and handed it to me. "For you and your brothers," he said. "The rest Natanis saves for the sick."

Gratefully I stowed the raccoon in my knapsack where it made a suspiciously large bulge. "Is Natanis here?" I asked.

Mike called the name. One of the Indians rose and came to us. He was rather tall for his people, with a broad, dignified face and dark, sparkling eyes.

There was need to make up to this ally for Arnold's suspicion of him, so I made a little speech. I said we were happy to see him, that he and his people had showed by their actions that they were our friends, and that I wanted him to talk with our Chief, Morgan. When Mike had translated, Natanis replied that he would be glad to do so.

I found Morgan a short way back in the woods, a gaunt, shaggy giant laden with the rifles and knapsacks of two men he was prodding ahead. He listened grimly while I told him what Natanis had been doing.

"I know," he said. "I've seen it. Tell him we thank him. How far is it to Sartignan? When can we get vittles?"

Natanis replied that Sartignan was two days away for well men, maybe longer for us. As to food, he believed it might come tomorrow, for he knew Arnold had already reached Sartignan.

"Tell him I'll see that Colonel Arnold knows all that's been done," said Morgan. "Tell him Arnold has had bad advice."

Natanis was pleased as we returned to the fire. He

pressed into my hand a small packet he took from a carry bag. Mike whispered that it was bear fat. That night I gave the raccoon to Lieutenant Humphrey for the company. Guiltily I saved the sustaining bear fat for our crew.

At dawn we again began our march, staggering as though drunk. Men fell in the snow and lay motionless until they were heaved up and driven forward.

Some time in the afternoon we heard yells and a spattering of gunshots. Aroused from stupor, we wiped gunlocks and began to load, for our first thought was of ambush. The uproar spread nearer. Soon we saw the reason for it. Plunging through the woods were three small beeves herded by trotting men—short, swarthy men in blanket coats and stocking caps who wore their hair in long queues. Behind these were three others on horseback, with bags of meal tied to their saddles. As he passed, one of the herdsmen pointed back with his stick and shouted something, as if urging us on.

Exultantly we shot off our rifles and raised shrill hunters' yells. Jerry shook his fist at the forest. "Ye won't get us now, ye devils," he bawled at the snow-laden trees.

There was a cluster of men around a fire. They were hacking at the carcass of a newly killed cow, skewering chunks of meat on ramrods and roasting them in the flames. Others, who were nearly barefoot, were cutting pieces of hide for moccasins. An open bag of coarse oaten meal stood against a tree.

We were still miles short of Sartignan, so after our feast we pushed on a while, camped, and the next day resumed the march. We passed a fall in the river which would have finished any boat surviving thus far, heavily wrested our feet through a long bog and crossed more hills. We forded an icy river, then an hour later another one—and so, at last, came to Sartignan.

It wasn't much of a place, an outpost of civilization. But its four whitewashed, thatch-roofed cottages and their barns seemed to us splendid. Indian tents were pitched beyond the cottages. A Frenchman was selling food to eager buyers who tried to communicate with him by sign language.

Caleb stepped up to the fellow and said something to him in his own tongue. After they'd jabbered a moment, Caleb, translating for the bunch of us, said the prices were pretty steep, so we'd best watch our shillings. Our crew ended up by buying three scrawny chickens and a parcel of eggs. The rest clamored for Caleb to keep on talking with the man.

When we got him away we demanded why he had never told us he spoke French. He laughed and said, "I don't much. Just enough to get by. In my sailing days I went to Quebec and to France, too. So I picked up a little of the lingo."

As we turned away with our purchases, Muskosis popped out of a tent. He was full of news. Arnold, he said, had set up headquarters in a village a few miles farther on. Tomorrow he would talk with the Abenakis and some Indians from this region. Misunderstandings would be resolved. There were no British soldiers in Quebec now, he continued; the Commander, General Carleton, had taken his small garrison to confront General Schuyler's Americans at Montreal, 170 miles up the St. Lawrence.

His next bit of information was less cheering. The Indians Arnold had sent to Quebec, Eneas and another, had returned. Eneas claimed they had been captured and Arnold's message had been taken. "Big lie," declared Mike. "Easy for our people to go to Quebec. English let us alone. Eneas takes English shillings."

"The skunk!" exclaimed Jerry. "They'll be fixin' for us."

"Would be anyway," said Caleb. "Those two spies."

Suddenly I understood what had happened.

"It's been two months since that pretending sutler took the message to Gage in Boston about this expedition," I said slowly, thinking it out. "That's time enough for Gage to do something about it if he could, but not time enough for the news to get to England, be acted on, and bring results in Quebec. Gage hoped the sutler could ruin our plans. That's why he was with us. He failed, but not by much. Now he's in Quebec."

Caleb nodded agreement. "We've got to get there before Carleton is called back. Quebec's a hard place to take if it's defended. A thing I'd like to know is what that blue-coat officer, who must be the boss spy, has been doing out West."

I was filled with cold rage at those men who had played such deviltry with two people who had come to them innocently asking for shoes. Ben had been much on my mind throughout the march. At times I had felt despondently there was small chance that he was in Quebec. At other times I had hoped.

Now we had come through from the brink of disaster. It seemed providential. Ben *must* be in Quebec. And we were going to take that place—if for no other reason than to get Ben out of prison and settle scores with the two men I continued to think of as the Hawk and the Bear.

8

FORTRESS QUEBEC

"So that's it."

There was a kind of wonder in the way Bill Riddle spoke, as if he could hardly believe we had at last reached our goal.

"That's Quebec," said Caleb with satisfaction.

" 'Tis a grand sight," murmured Jerry, then added rather doubtfully, "but I'm thinking it looks hard and cold, as if it didn't give two pins for us."

Our shivering company, ankle-deep in fresh-fallen snow, stood on the bank at the village of Levis above the wind-ruffled St. Lawrence. On the river, seemingly small because of distance, were two British warships. Staring curiously at the lofty headland across the mile-wide barrier of water, I understood what Jerry meant. Quebec stood proud and aloof.

Along the river's edge at the base of the rock stretched a narrow jumble of gray stone houses. Back of their roofs rose the cliff of a plateau on which dwelling houses clustered around several large buildings—spired churches and monasteries and government structures. At one place a narrow street, lined with houses, climbed a steep slope from the lower to the upper town. The whole plateau rose gradually from its wedgelike point overlooking the tributary St. Charles River to the westerly height of Cape Diamond, towering 300 feet above the St. Lawrence.

"It's a strong place," said Caleb with grudging admiration. "The land side is protected by a thick stone wall and a dry moat, and the cliff pretty well takes care of the river side."

"Where was it General Wolfe got up that cliff to take it from the French?" inquired Peter Anderson.

Caleb pointed up the river to a spot beyond Cape Diamond. "There's a little cove up their where he climbed at night to the Plains of Abraham. He'd been trying to take the town from the St. Charles side, over there, but he couldn't. The French Governor had been pestering General Montcalm to go out and fight, so when Wolfe got on the Plains, Montcalm did. In the open, a few rounds by the English knocked out the French. Both generals got killed, you know. That was sixteen years ago. I've always believed if Montcalm had stayed behind his walls he could have laughed at the British."

Someone voiced the opinion that since there were no soldiers there—as we then believed—we ought somehow to get across fast and scare the people into opening the gates.

If appearances could do it we were well qualified to turn the trick. We were the worst bunch of rag-tags ever seen in anything calling itself an army. Our tattered garments were held together with strings and strips of blanket. Our long, matted hair mingled with beards, most of them fuzzily young, that grew on our pinched faces. Altogether, we were a wolfish, wild-eyed crew.

The seventy-five miles across the flat Canadian plain from Sartignan had been made in four days, with a forced march through half of last night. We had slept nights in the houses and barns of Canadian villages, each dominated by its church. Some of our poor fellows, Captain Dearborn among them, had been so sick they had been left in the care of friendly French habitants. Many others were dragging along at a pace slower than we had set.

From Mike I learned that Arnold had met with the Abenakis and some Canadian Indians who were not sure which side to choose. Now knowing the truth, he had praised Natanis and the Abenakis for their help. He had enlisted them and some of the Canadian Indians as paid scouts, which greatly pleased them. It showed Arnold could change his mind if proved wrong, a thing not every man can do.

Now we looked at our prize, so tantalizingly near but still beyond our grasp. British sailors had stripped this south shore of all boats they could find. We would have to cross the river in canoes, when enough were collected, and we would have to do it at night, for by day the British ships could blast us to pieces. To worsen matters, a strong, cold north wind was kicking up whitecaps on the St. Lawrence, making a crossing by canoes too risky to attempt.

Having taken possession of a warehouse and some other buildings, we fretted and froze for several days while most of the stragglers arrived. Arnold commandeered some log dugouts from owners who had hidden them. During this time of waiting an Indian brought a message from General Richard Montgomery, who had succeeded the ailing General Schuyler as commander in the west. It informed Arnold that the Americans were closing in on Montreal. But we learned, too, that the British had by no means been idle. For this, no doubt, we could thank Brownbeard's message to Gage, and Eneas's trip to Quebec.

One of Arnold's Quebec friends, a merchant named Halstead, had slipped up river from the Isle of Orleans with news that 150 troops from Newfoundland and a British frigate had arrived a few days ahead of us. Later, a Canadian deserter told us that more reinforcements—170 men under a Colonel Allen McLean—had escaped Montgomery's trap at Montreal and had just reached the city. Time was fast running out.

But at last luck smiled on us. On November 13th, the sixth day at Levis, the wind dropped. Hastily we made ready for the crossing. Indians had brought canoes from the Chaudière. With these and the dugouts we had thirty-five craft.

At ten o'clock of that black, freezing night we gathered at the river bank. Arnold gave each company instructions. The distance was more than two miles up river on a slanting course. The boats could hold only two paddlers and four or five passengers, with their share of the stores that remained, so there would be several trips. We must make no noise. If fortune was with us we might have Quebec by dawn. It was a desperate venture, but we were desperate and more than ready to chance it.

Arnold and Morgan were in the first canoe to push off. Caleb and I seized paddles and soon after followed with our passengers, keeping close to the craft ahead lest we lose it in the dark. Behind, other canoes followed in single file. The St. Lawrence was still a-surge in the aftermath of the gale. You felt as if you were riding up and down in a strange black void where the only points of reference were the tossing canoe ahead and a few dim lights along the Quebec shore.

After nearly an hour of paddling we beached the canoe softly on a graveled bank. "Wolfe's cove," murmured Caleb. Our passengers got out and we headed back for Point Levis. The second trip was completed without incident, but the third was more precarious. The moon was up, the wind was rising, and the cloud cover was beginning to break.

We were in midstream when I heard subdued sounds ahead. Soon we found that an overburdened canoe had broken in two. The people who had been in it were threshing about trying to keep afloat in the icy water. Our passengers clutched three of them and another boat got the remainder, and we towed them ashore as fast as we could, and built a fire to keep them from freezing. The last of the flotilla reached the cove by four o'clock. Left behind were about a hundred men under Captain Hanchet, some of them invalids. These crossed later.

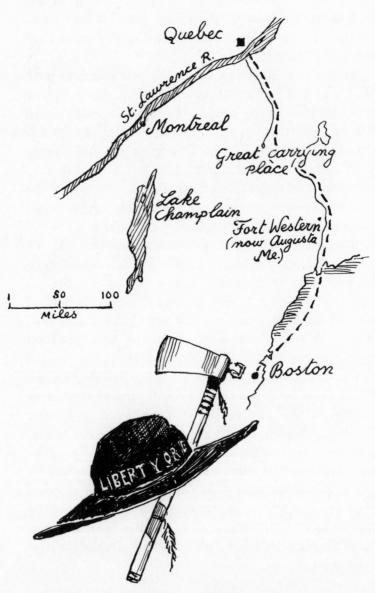

Quebec

St. Lawrence R.

Montreal

Great carrying place

Lake Champlain

Fort Western (now Augusta Me.)

1 50 100
Miles

Boston

LIBERTY OR DEATH

Arnold's Route North

We climbed a path up the cliff and came out on a snow-covered plain. Dimly discerned figures formed in companies were tramping back and forth trying to keep warm. They were waiting, we learned, for a report from a party which had been sent to reconnoiter the city.

The group returned before dawn. They had been the length of the wall and among some deserted houses outside the gates. The wall was guarded lightly, if at all. But the gates were closed and barred.

At the first gray of daylight some men were picked as advance guards and sent toward Quebec to watch the gates and cut off roads into the city. The rest of us set off in the direction of some dwellings in the distance. The first one we came to was a large wooden house surrounded by outbuildings and barns. Here we found some fellows loading carts with joints of meat, bedding, furniture, and other stuff from the house, which belonged, they told us, to a bigwig, a Major Caldwell, now safe in Quebec. The men, who were his servants, were trying to save some of their master's property.

This gave us the first laugh we'd had all night. Happily we helped them put the things back where they belonged. Then we ransacked the house, stoked up the stoves, helped ourselves to bread, butter, and beef, and went to sleep.

Some time after noon we were awakened by an alarm that the Redcoats were coming out to attack. Grabbing our rifles, we ran toward the city. In the distance we could see the walls and, beyond, the roofs of the upper town silhouetted against the sky.

From this elevated plain Quebec did not look like the cliff-crowning fortress we had gazed at from Point Levis. Outside the walls were suburbs of small houses clustered around the three gates of St. Johns, St. Louis, and the Palace Gate, the latter suburb, named St. Roque, being down the slope towards the St. Charles River.

The cause of the alarm was revealed by one of our guards. A party of Redcoats had sortied from St. Johns gate and taken a captive, one of Morgan's men who had been posted near the cluster of houses outside the gate. He had probably fallen asleep from weariness. They had hustled him into the city.

Arnold formed all the companies beyond musket shot and paraded us up and down the length of the wall facing the plain, a distance of somewhat less than a mile. Soldiers huzzahed defiance from the ramparts and a number of cannon were fired, which did no harm to us. But if Arnold had hoped to stir the British into coming out to fight, he was disappointed. Later, an officer was sent with a white flag to demand surrender. As he neared the gate a big cannon ball whizzed over his head. Clearly whoever was in charge of Quebec was no faintheart to be bluffed into submission.

This was typical of the futility of our first try at taking Quebec—without cannon, without scaling ladders, without much of anything except our rifles and muskets and the rags that barely covered our shivering bodies.

The company moved out of its comfortable quarters in Caldwell's manor house to take possession of the general hospital, a long, gloomy stone building where some twenty nuns attended the sick of the city and adjoining area. It was located below the plateau, beside the St. Charles, about a mile from the city walls. We occupied a nearby log building.

On the second night of our stay here Jerry and I and another of our company named John Kurts went on guard duty at midnight near the St. Roque suburb, which lay under the walls about midway between St. Johns Gate and Palace Gate, at a point where the wall turned at right angles to top the cliff above the St. Charles. Our purpose was to stop wagons with supplies from entering the city from the St. Charles ferry. We had a lantern shielded by a dark cloth.

After four or five hours our teeth were chattering. We had been stamping our feet to warm them when suddenly we heard a softly whistled tune, then the crunch of approaching steps. We wheeled toward the sound, rifles ready. A moment passed and we made out, near at hand, a figure coming from the direction of the wall. "Halt," I commanded quietly. Beside me, Jerry's rifle clicked to the cock. The whistling stopped.

" 'Allo," said a cheerful voice. "Americans, yes? Good. Pray have care with the muskets."

"Come closer," I ordered. Kurts picked up the lantern, raised the cloth, and threw the light on the stranger. He was wearing a white blanket coat and a furred cap. In a brief glimpse before the cloth was dropped I saw a smiling young face.

"Who are you? What are you doing here?"

"My name is Jean Claude Merault," was the reply. "I am of Quebec. I wish to see your *commandant*. It is truly of importance."

"What is it?" countered Jerry suspiciously.

"What I have to tell you is this: The *Anglais* know you have no cannon. They believe you also lack ammunition. They are preparing their field pieces. They plan to come out and attack soon, thinking to beat you before the arrival of your General Montgomery. McLean is a determined man. It is vairy serious, really."

Aside from his French accent, he spoke like an educated Englishman.

"Why do you tell us this?" I asked. "What is it to you?"

"Me, I am *Français,* that is why. I do not like the *Anglais.* I was young when they took Canada, but I remain *Canadien Français.* You fight them. I wish to help ––for the liberty of Canada."

A brief silence followed. I was uncertain. I believed he was telling the truth, but how to be sure?

"Could be the British sent him," muttered Jerry.

It was possible. Yet Morgan should hear his story. "One of us must take him to Dan," I said.

"You go. John and I will be relieved soon anyway."

On the way to our barracks I questioned the stranger. How had he managed to get out of the city?

"It is nothing," he answered with assurance. "There are ways. I come and go as I please. This time by the lower town, under the cliff, past the Intendant's Palace —and I am here."

I asked about Quebec, the garrison, the state of the people.

He said there were between 800 and 900 troops and sailors, well armed. More than 100 guns were mounted on the walls and there were some twenty field pieces. It was a small garrison to guard the length of the wall, but sufficient against us. As for the inhabitants, the few who were English would fight. So would the organized Canadian militia. And he admitted sadly that not many of the French inhabitants could be counted on to help us. "Some, if they had the chance," he said. "But most are like cows. They prefer to be left alone."

I was curious to know how he happened to speak English so well. "I set myself quite early to learn it," he replied. "That is but logical for one of a conquered people, is it not? It is a way to advancement—and other things. One knows what is going on. It was not difficult," he added carelessly. "I have a gift for it. I also speak Huron and some Iroquois."

During the walk I had considered a question that I hardly dared ask for fear of disappointment. Now I came out with it. "Are there any American prisoners in Quebec?"

"Yes. Not many, perhaps thirty. They are held in a small prison near Les Jesuites, a monastery. I have a friend whose job it is to bring them food."

I hesitated. "Do you know their names?" I asked softly. "Is there one called Ben Donaldson?"

He replied that he did not know but that it should be easy to learn through his friend. He repeated the name to memorize it. I told him my name and he repeated that, then chuckled. "He is a *camarade*, eh? Rest assured, my friend Daveed, I will look into the matter."

Although it was still dark when we reached the barrack, the company was up and about breakfast. The

French boy repeated to Morgan what he had told me. Big Dan questioned Jean Claude thoroughly and seemed satisfied. "Arnold heard a rumor yesterday from one of his friends. This ought to fortify it."

The interview with Arnold that morning I did not hear, but it seemed to bring results. When Jean Claude emerged from headquarters he said he was going back to Quebec. I urged him to wait until night but he said he knew a safe way by a path under the Cape Diamond redoubt. We parted with a warm handshake. He spoke Ben's name again. "It is a long chance," he murmured, "but we learn. I will see you again when possible." He strode off across the snow-carpeted Plains of Abraham.

That afternoon a general inventory of arms and ammunition was ordered. The result was a shock. Because of losses from Dead River on, soakings, and other causes, there was left in reserve only enough usable powder for four rounds per man. We were almost equally low on lead for balls. There was murmuring as to why this state of affairs hadn't been discovered sooner. Plainly it would be foolish now to try to meet an assault from Quebec.

A decision was soon made. Before dawn next morning the companies were mustered and the little army set off up the St. Lawrence toward a place called Pointe-aux-Trembles, twenty miles from Quebec. There we would await General Montgomery's arrival from Montreal with cannon, ammunition, warm clothing, and other captured stores.

9

HEARTBREAKING SIEGE

Pointe-aux-Trembles, meaning "Aspen Point," was so named because of the large number of aspens growing along the river there, whose leaves in the summer, one side green and the other silver, shimmered in the sun with the slightest breeze. Here we got to know better the village farmers of Canada. The settlement was a straggling collection of houses stretching a mile along the road to Montreal, with a spacious Roman Catholic church in its midst.

Jerry, Caleb, Solomon, Bill Riddle and I were billeted with a family named Bruiac, consisting of a gnarled little man in his thirties, his buxom, cheerful wife—both inveterate pipe smokers—a daughter of fourteen, and two younger brothers. After a day of strained observation and evident worry by the Bruiacs about what these ferocious-looking foreigners might take it into their heads to do, we began to get along very well with them.

The Bruiac house was protected from wintry gales by banked earth and snowdrifts outside, and inside by strips of paper pasted over every crack by which air could enter. It was heated by an iron stove in the general room next to the kitchen, which was also where we slept. Here at last we felt comfortably warm, but when we had to go outside in our thin garments the contrast was too great. Soon we were all coughing and sniffling with colds.

These people seemed to live fairly well despite the rigors of their climate. They had plenty of beef and pork, cut into chunks and kept in a cold storeroom. Unplucked fowls hung from rafters in the unheated attic, and in the cellar under the kitchen were quantities of cabbages, potatoes, onions, and turnips. In the evening Madame Bruiac and her daughter prepared the next day's dinner by putting pieces of meat, along with vegetables, in a pot of water with salt and various herbs added. The covered pot simmered during the night on the stove. In the morning it was taken off and the stew was cooked in the kitchen fireplace until noon, when it was served with slices of crusty bread. We gained favor by adding our own meat allotments to the common pot.

General Montgomery had taken Montreal while we were still before Quebec. Now Arnold dispatched Aaron Burr with a message for the General. Burr chose to disguise himself as a priest. Speaking French and no doubt showering blessings on all and sundry, he completed the assignment safely. The whole expedition eagerly awaited the arrival of Montgomery and his captured goods.

But we Morgan men were not to witness the junction here. After eight days at Pointe-aux-Trembles we were given extra supplies of powder and shot from the small amounts left and were ordered back to mount guard on Quebec. We parted from the Bruiacs with mutual expressions of esteem.

We reached St. Foy at dark and pressed on to the log barrack near the hospital. Morgan was eager to start pecking at the British on the wall, so we moved up to the edge of St. Roque and lodged in houses near a tavern run by a man named Menut.

Between us and the city were the cottages and cabins of St. Roque and then, nestled under the slope when the wall turned at right angles, was a big, barnlike structure of stone. This, it was said, had been used by a notorious French Intendant, or governor, before the British took Quebec, to store goods bought at his own prices which he sold at extortionate profit to the poverty-stricken Canadians. It was called La Friponne, meaning "The Cheat."

A hundred yards beyond this stood the impressive stone building that had been the Intendant's Palace and, still further along, a path mounted to the Palace Gate. After the Gate the way narrowed between the cliff and the mud banks bordering the St. Charles. It was by this shelf overhung by battlements that one reached the lower town. La Friponne and the Palace were excellent for our purpose. From them we could shoot up at sentries as they passed gunports and the British could not shoot back without leaning over the parapet, which they soon found to be unhealthy.

By now a cold as of the polar regions had settled over the land. I have heard it said that at such temperatures it is too cold to snow, but that was not so here. The stuff continued to come down, sometimes in brief flurries, sometimes for hours on end. We were glad when, after several days, General Montgomery and his men, with Arnold's companies, arrived before Quebec.

General Montgomery was originally from Ireland. He had won honors as a British officer in the Seven Years War with France. After the war he had resigned his commission, had come to the colonies, and had married a daughter of the wealthy Robert Livingston of New York. He had wished for a quiet life at his estate on the Hudson but at the first flame of revolt he had joined the colonists and had been commissioned a brigadier general under Philip Schuyler, whose estate was near Saratoga on the Hudson. When the latter had to quit, he took over. The new commander was tall and soldierlike. He inspired confidence, for he looked as though he knew his business.

The same could not be said for some of those he brought with him. He had left garrisons at St. Johns and Montreal, so his force was reduced to about 300 New Yorkers. Aside from the efficient artillery company under a Captain Lamb, these seemed to lack the spring and spirit of good soldiers. With them and 200 Canadian militia who had joined us, the army now numbered 1,100.

Now clothes and ammunition arrived. Most of them were from British stores taken at St. Johns—shoes, woolen stockings, mittens, and, best of all, blanket coats. The men joked about wearing lobsterback uniforms, but they put them on just the same.

We were now aided by a number of pieces of artillery. They included some mortars that shot shells up to arch down and fall within the city walls. Others were cannon for firing solid shot at the walls. But all were of disappointingly small size. It was decided to emplace a battery on the Plains of Abraham 700 yards from St. Johns Gate. Because of the frozen earth this called for construction of a number of gabions, large cylinders of woven birch branches, which were filled with snow on which water was poured. In the near-zero temperature the mixture quickly became solid ice. Five of our largest guns were wheeled up to the icy embrasures and the shooting began.

Both before and after the clothing issue we riflemen had continued to crack away at the British sentries from La Friponne. Soon the British tried countermeasures. From mortars inside Quebec they threw huge 13-inch bombshells to land on the slope above us and roll down and explode against the walls of our fortress, which fortunately were five feet thick. Because of the danger in passing back and forth by daylight we had taken to staying two or three days at a time, sleeping in La Friponne at night.

One night I was taking my turn at guard duty while the others slept, when the British loosed one of their monsters at us. It hit the stone wall outside the exact spot where Jerry was snoozing. The explosion was tremendous. Jerry leaped high in the air and came down running. He was outside the building plowing desperately through a snowdrift when I caught up with him. I shook him back to his senses and he began to babble, "W-wh-what-what happened?" When we got back inside the others roared with laughter. But Jerry saw nothing funny in it.

Ever since our return from Pointe-aux-Trembles I had been impatiently awaiting word from Jean Claude. On December 21st there was a heavy snow. In its wake Jean Claude turned up at Menut's tavern inquiring for me. As I was off duty I hastened to join him. His eyes were sparkling.

" 'Allo, Daveed," he smiled. "It is good to see all is well with you." He went on with a rush, "Now contain yourself, my friend. Do not become excited. I have news. Your comrade is in Quebec."

I gave a great shout of joy that turned all eyes in the tavern on us. It was unbelievable. "You're sure?" I demanded.

"Of the greatest certainty. I have seen him and talked with him. My friend at the prison contrived that I should take his place for a day. Your friend is eagerly awaiting you and the rest. He looks well, though I think he could eat more than he gets."

As we celebrated over rum punch, Jean Claude described the house in which Ben and the other prisoners were kept and told me how to reach it. Neither of us then felt any doubt that the Americans would take Quebec. Jean Claude had something else on his mind and in the course of our talk he came to it. It had puzzled him. After hearing from Ben how he had been captured, he had thought about it a good deal. The gist of the matter was that there was an American in Quebec who seemed to have much influence with Governor Carleton—at least he was believed to be

American. He had come with Carleton down the St. Lawrence after our capture of Montreal.

"What does he look like?"

"Rather tall. Thin face. Big hooked nose like the beak of a hawk. Cold gray eyes."

The description was pat. I whistled in surprise. Did he have a companion, a big, thickset fellow with a beard? Jean Claude had not seen such a one. I told him what had happened after Ben's capture, how I had later recognized the other spy on the river, and how I had escaped his Indians. He listened intently.

"When you come into Quebec we must make sure the big nose does not escape, and we must find the other one," he murmured.

Tension rose among the besiegers of Fortress Quebec. Everyone sensed that the time was nearing for the try at capture. For one thing, most of the New Englanders' enlistments would run out at the end of the year, and while Dearborn's and several other companies could be counted on to remain, there was open disaffection among others. Also, it was now clear that we would never take Quebec by battering at its walls with the cannon we had. The ice fort had been too weak to stand against the weight of enemy round shot; it had been virtually abandoned after men had been killed there. Montgomery had decided that the only chance for victory was to storm the city at night.

Near sundown on Christmas day Montgomery reviewed Arnold's command and made a short, sensible speech pointing out the necessity for that course. He asked if we agreed. The rifle companies shouted yes, and so did the musketmen, though in the case of some of the latter there seemed to be little enthusiasm.

The General convened a meeting with his officers and a plan of attack was agreed upon. Later, Captain Smith, ever talkative and boastful, and over drinks at the tavern, told the plan in the hearing of a score of men. The next day it was all over camp. That night one of the New Yorkers deserted to the British. Smith might as well have told Carleton himself.

There was snow on the 27th. We prepared for the attack, but the storm slackened and the thing was called off. Two days of more or less clear weather followed. The British threw a lot of cannon balls at us. They seemed in a state of nerves.

On December 30th the day was generally sunny, but cloud streaks formed high in the sky. After dark thicker clouds obscured the moon. Around midnight snow, driven by a piercing, howling northeast wind, began flailing us slantwise in the force of ice pellets.

At four o'clock in the morning we were routed out by Morgan. We picked up the long pikes with sharpened points that had been made for every fourth man, and the scaling ladders, one for each twenty men, and formed lines. We tried to protect our rifle locks from the storm by cuddling them under our blanket coats. We knew what we were to do.

While the Canadian militia and a small Massachusetts detachment made a demonstration before the St. Johns Gate with fireballs and noise to distract attention, Montgomery and his York troops were to take a guardhouse and barricade under Cape Diamond (instead of the ones at Cape Diamond, as had originally been planned). Simultaneously, we were to get into the lower town by the narrow way between the cliff and the St. Charles and storm the barricades there. Then we were to meet Montgomery's men, coming from the opposite direction, and together push on into the upper town. The signal for the joint attack was to be a rocket lofted from the Plains of Abraham.

We began to move out between the battered houses of St. Roque. I noticed that Daniel Morgan was in regular uniform and was wearing his sword, a thing he seldom did.

10

IN DESPERATE BATTLE

Of all the snowstorms we had endured, this seemed the worst, perhaps because we were so laden with burdens, so taxed by struggles through massive drifts, and so confused by the dark and the gale-driven flakes. I had a panic feeling that we might be smothered by the sheer force of the storm and lie buried under a white mound the rest of the winter.

We had not yet reached La Friponne when our two lines were opened so that Arnold, his secretary Oswald, several aides, and a small party of musketmen could pass between and take the lead. Arnold, his voice lowered to a cautious level, was saying: "This is the time, boys. This is the time. We're going to take this blasted place. You're good fighters. Now's the time to show it. Follow me."

Behind Arnold's group came Lamb's artillerymen straining at ropes as they slowly dragged a small gun on a sledge. Their intent was to blast open the two barricades in the lower town. When they had passed, Morgan ordered us on. Behind us were the remaining companies of Arnold's command.

We slipped and slid and plowed through the snow in silence, past the Intendant's Palace and on another 200 yards or more until we came to the path that mounted to the Palace Gate. Then we halted and melted into single file to negotiate the narrowing way we must travel to get to the lower town.

On our right were deep drifts swept up against a row of warehouses that lined the foot of the cliff. On our left were jagged ice cakes pushed up from the St. Charles by winter gales. At places we had to clamber over them, occasionally taking a tumble. Carrying rifles, pikes, and ladders, the passage was hard.

There are those who say they saw the signal rocket for the joint attack at five o'clock of that black, tempestuous night. Perhaps because I was concentrating on peering down rather than up, I did not. But I know that we were slowly struggling on when artillery suddenly crashed on the heights above, lighting the sky with flashes. Muskets began to pop and a wild clanging of church bells broke out in the upper town.

"Oh, oh!" yelped Jerry. "Now they know about us for sure."

In the midst of the uproar the head of the column came to a stop. Rocket fireballs arched above us to fall in the snow, where they continued to blaze with eery red flames, lighting up the whole wild scene. What with the fireballs, the flashes from guns and muskets, and the continuous din, the scene took on a semblance to the mouth of hell which our pastor back home could so vividly describe when in the mood to preach a sinner's sermon. Bullets flicked past with sharp, whirring sounds.

"What's holding us up?" demanded Solomon.

We tried firing back at the flashes above—and made the horrid discovery that our rifles wouldn't shoot. Powder and locks and the insides of barrels had been damped by the driving snow. Morgan came back from whatever he had been doing ahead and ordered us on. With what speed we could make we crowded after him.

Soon we saw the reason for the halt. The sledge on which Captain Lamb's small cannon had been set was stuck in a big snowdrift. Artillerymen were digging around it and prying at it with levers like frantic ants, but to no avail. We passed it and went on.

"We'll have to take those barricades barehanded," mumbled Caleb. One of our fellows dropped into the snow with a faint gurgling sound. Growls of frustration broke from the line. We rounded the point and came into a narrow street of the lower town. We had gone but a few steps when with a great explosion and flash of fire a cannon at the first barricade blasted us with grapeshot. Several men fell.

"Quick," yelled Arnold, "take that barricade!"

A rattle of musketry came from houses on both sides of the street. I heard Arnold swear. To my astonishment he was down in the snow. Those around him paused uncertainly, shocked by his fall. "I'm hit in the leg," he said after a moment. "Help me up. I've got to stand."

If there was uncertainty in the minds of his aides there was none in the mind of our commander. Hoisted to stand on his sound leg, his arms draped over the shoulders of two aides, he spoke urgently. "Don't worry about this. Get on, boys, Get on. Drive them from it. Take over, Morgan."

"Let's go, men," bawled Morgan. "Get the ladder here." He ran toward the obstruction and we raced after him while Arnold shouted encouragement.

Ladders were quickly placed against the face of the barricade. Morgan scrambled up. As many as could find foothold mounted behind him. As we toppled over the defense we fell into snow on a gun platform. By the light of a lantern the fleeing British had left we saw them scattering, some running up the street, others piling into a house alongside the barricade. We snapped our useless rifles at them. Through all of this pre-dawn fight Morgan seemed to bear a charmed life, as if fate had marked him for better things, which may have been so, considering the part he was to play later in the war.

"Take after them up the street," he commanded half the company now gathered around him. "Pin 'em against the houses. Don't let 'em get to the next barrier. Heth, take the rest and bust into that house. Use pikes and gun butts. Get their muskets." He went pounding up the street, followed by a keening pack.

We broke the windows of the house beside the barricade and got among the holed-up British. "Drop your arms if you want quarter," bawled Lieutenant Heth. Some tried to fight. Others tried to escape. Two were skewered on pikes. Most of them hastily surrendered. We seized their dry muskets which they had had no time to reload, and some ammunition, and herded the prisoners into the street. Leaving a small guard over

them, we plunged on after Morgan. By the time we caught up, fifty scared, befuddled Redcoats were backed against walls, hands above their heads.

As we approached the second barricade we ran a gantlet of musketry. It was inaccurate because they were shooting with only the light of their own flashes to go by, but we took no chances. Crouching against the fronts of houses, we plodded on carefully, thrusting our muskets through panes of glass and firing at those within. More prisoners came tumbling out.

By this time many of the New Englanders who had been strung out behind us had arrived. Grimly and efficiently they helped clean out and disarm pockets of snipers. Men from various companies joined us in pouring a hot fire at the second barrier. This had been built where the narrow street divided into two streets, one of which led to the approach to the upper town. According to plan, we were to capture this barricade and join Montgomery's troops beyond it, at a point where a flight of steps led to Mountain Street and up to the heart of Quebec.

The fact that we were not cannonaded here was probably due to our own firing. The defenders seemed to lose heart quickly—for a time at least. Someone found a sally port open. Morgan ordered us to stay where we were and keep the prisoners together. Then he took an interpreter and went through the opening to investigate. Above us the cannon continued to boom.

Now the situation was complicated by an outpouring of French men, women, and children from the houses along the narrow street. Some fled through the barrier to the upper town. Others milled about hysterically imploring protection. What had been confusion became chaos.

Somehow we sifted most of the British prisoners from the French inhabitants and got the latter out of the way, which was not easy in the darkness. We were still at the task when Morgan returned. He seemed bemused, uncertain yet excited. He collected as many of the New England officers as he could quickly find. I heard him tell them: "Montgomery is not up yet. There's no sign of him. But I think the British are demoralized. The way seems clear to the upper town. I'm for going on now, without General Montgomery. It's our chance. We'd better grasp it."

More cautious officers—some of whom outranked Big Dan—voiced opposition to the daring idea. It was pointed out that Morgan would be disobeying orders if he didn't wait for Montgomery. And anyway our prisoners must now nearly outnumber us; it would be foolhardy to leave them unguarded in our rear. Faced with such arguments, Morgan hesitated.

And then, suddenly, it was too late. The British, got in hand by some capable leader, came belting back, closed the sally port, and sprayed us with canister from two cannon behind the barrier. Packed in that alley of a street, we suffered.

Morgan raged. "Get ladders here quick! Scatter out!" Some of our fellows lay motionless in the snow. Lieutenant Humphrey, brave and gallant as always, tried to scale the barricade but was hit by a musket ball and instantly killed. Captain Lamb of the York artillery lost part of his face to a burst of grapeshot. We fired at the portholes as fast as we could, and with effect, for the cannon fire stopped. But then the British worked their way from the barrier to the upper floor of houses above us and poured on us a converging fire.

In the graying dawn we took refuge on the ground floors of the stone houses and kept shooting through the still-falling snow at any enemies we could spot. But it was a losing battle, and at last we realized it. Men began to growl, "We've been sold."

After the new attack many of our prisoners had escaped. They had somehow rearmed themselves and now, in the growing light, these began to harry us from the direction of the first barricade. Captain Hendricks, firing at them from a window, was hit. He fell back on the floor, shot through the heart.

Now a new, ominous outburst of musketry was heard from the direction of the St. Charles. Jerry cocked his ear at it. "I'll bet they've come down from the Palace Gate," he muttered. "If that's it, we're in a real bad fix. Hemmed in on both sides."

We held out for another hour or so as our enemies grew constantly stronger in numbers and in confidence. Ammunition was running low. Groups of Americans were cut off and taken prisoner. The British cautiously moved up to the houses we occupied. An officer shouted a demand to surrender. Morgan drew his sword. The muscles of his jaw worked convulsively. "I've missed our chance," he said. "I should have gone on."

He stepped into the street. A ring of bayonets threatened him. A Redcoat soldier tried to wrest his sword from him. Morgan's left fist smashed the man back. There were tears of rage in his eyes. He saw a robed priest standing back of the clustered British and beckoned to him. "I'll surrender my sword to you," he said, "but not to these cowardly scoundrels."

The astonished priest came forward, inclined his head gravely, and took the sword.

Only after we were taken prisoners—some four hundred of us, including wounded—did we learn why Montgomery had not joined us. That brave, able general had led his troops along a narrow path by the river below Cape Diamond, and had passed two deserted barriers. His men, feeling their way along the slippery way under the precipice, had straggled badly. Montgomery had waited before the next barrier for them to catch up. Then, helping to tear down the barrier with his own hands, he had reached a blockhouse with two cannon in it, intending to go on some three quarters of a mile under the cliff to the appointed meeting place.

That was not to be. As Montgomery approached the blockhouse a gun, manned by sailors, fired a charge of canister which killed him and four of his men. Unnerved by this misfortune, Colonel Donald Campbell, second in command, had failed his duty. He had given up the attack, leaving the British to throw all their forces at us. By blind chance America had lost a first-rate leader—and Quebec as well.

It would be hard to imagine a more dejected lot of prisoners. All our toil and privations had gone for nothing. Far from freeing Ben, I was now a fellow captive. And in this proud and hateful town, somewhere close to its Governor Carleton, lurked the malignant figure of the man in the blue coat.

Yet so tough is the human spirit that even now not all was blackness. Jerry, sensing how it was with me, said: "Cheer up, Dave. While there's life there's hope, as the feller said when he stood on the gallows." And Caleb, that stout heart, added: "He's right. This war is just beginning. There'll be better times later on."

II

A HARD WINTER

Sir Guy Carleton, Governor
of Canada, was from a line of English gentry who had
come to Ireland and taken possession of Irish land. He
was handsome in an angular, horsy way, with a strong
face and thoughtful eyes. He was an efficient and sometimes stern man but, as we were to learn, humane as
well. Yet being a prisoner is hard under any circumstances, and ours were poor.

The wounded were taken to a hospital. The officers
were confined in the Seminary, a large building adjacent to the Cathedral. The rest of us were penned in an
upper floor of a monastery called the Recollets, a big
stone structure surrounding a little garden now deep
in snow. We were crammed into small rooms 10 by 12
feet in size, ten of us to each of them. We were
crowded, but that helped to keep us warm, for the
rooms were unheated and the stove in the hall between
rows of rooms didn't throw its warmth very far.

Carleton gave General Montgomery, his onetime
friend in the British army, and the other officers a mili-

tary funeral with all honors. He also sent a flag of truce to Arnold—in the hospital beside the St. Charles where he grimly hung on with the rest of his men—offering to take whatever small possessions we had left behind that might help us live more tolerably.

It was different with Colonel McLean, the one who had hurried back to Quebec with reinforcements at the crucial moment, who came among us soon afterward. He was a dour old Scotsman who made no bones about hating us rebels. His purpose was to find among the prisoners those who had been born in Great Britain. A good many, mostly from Ireland, admitted they had come from the Old Country. To these McLean gave the choice of enlisting in a British "emigrant's" regiment or being tried for treason in London. All told, some ninety of our fellows enlisted, fearing they would be hanged. But under the circumstances they swore allegiance to the Crown with tongue in cheek, determined to desert at the first chance.

Soon after this, Governor Carleton came to the Recollets to inspect our quarters. With him was a man in civilian clothes. I got one glimpse of his profile, then turned my back and moved behind Caleb. There was no doubt of it; Carleton's companion was the spy I had last seen as he left General Washington's headquarters. Carleton merely paused at the doorway, asked a few not unfriendly questions, and went on. But I was to live now in constant fear.

The short days and long nights slowly passed. The weather was bitter cold. We had enough to eat to keep body and soul together, but little more. The daily ra-

tion was two or three biscuits, a tiny piece of fat pork
or salt beef, a cup of gluey rice, and a little rancid
butter. Occasionally we got some molasses. The cooking was done in two large copper kettles by a man from
a New England company.

It was here that I learned to like, or at least tolerate,
lobscouse, a dish made by stewing our vile biscuits with
a little water in tin pots on the stove until we had a
paste, then adding grease from the cook's boiling of
pork. After more stewing, two or three spoonfuls of
molasses were stirred into the mess. It was remarkably
filling.

Time passed slowly. Some sat and moped. Others
talked of their families and friends, chewing over each
precious memory. Caleb sought to relieve tedium by
teaching his fragmentary French to any who would
make the effort to learn. And there were the inveterate
gamblers who managed to procure a pack of cards and
spent hours playing for biscuits in lieu of the money no
one had.

Escape had been on our minds from the beginning,
but the possibilities were bad. Although we had the run
of the rooms and the hall, two guards were stationed
day and night at the stairs and others were on the floor
below. In addition, sentry boxes had been set at several
points around the building, and storm lanterns
mounted on poles lighted the scene at night. The
guards were cheerful, fairly decent fellows on the
whole, but they did their duty. That we found one
exception made no difference in the end.

On a blustery day in early February one of the

guards, whose name I never knew, walked slowly by me as I stood near the stove in the hall. He stared at me intently, then brushed against me and slipped a piece of paper in my hand. My thoughts were in a whirl as I went to my cubbyhole and darted a glance at the small writing of the message. It read:

Have plan for B. night Feb. 18. Tell me your situation that I may know what to do. Trust bearer. He is well paid. Destroy this. J.C.

Considering what to reply, it seemed that even Jean Claude would find the Recollets a tough nut to crack. It would take time to prepare an escape and the co-ordination inside and out would have to be perfect. Also, I would not leave without my four companions, which made it harder.

I showed the note to my teammates. We agreed on a reply, which I wrote on a page from Caleb's notebook with quill and ink he was allowed for his French lessons. I set forth the difficulties, stressed the need for exact timing, and urged Jean Claude to attend first to Ben's escape. There was no reply, and I never saw the guard again. Perhaps he had been frightened or had been transferred to other duties. At any event, I heard nothing from Jean Claude during the rest of the winter.

Smallpox broke out. Some prisoners never returned from the hospital. Our prison ranks were refilled, however, by the return of most of those who had been forced to take the King's service. So many had gotten away and so many others had tried to that they were no longer considered of any value. They said Arnold was clinging to the siege with the New Yorkers, some Canadians, and a few New Englanders who had escaped the trap at the Palace Gate.

On March 15, while Quebec was still in the grip of winter, we were transferred to the Dauphin jail, a "bombproof" stone structure 300 yards from the St. Johns Gate, which we could see clearly because there were no buildings directly between it and the jail. The jail stood on sloping ground and beneath the first floor was a cellar with one end below ground and the other, facing a street, above ground. Morgan's men took one of the eight large rooms on the first floor. We were now so reduced by killed and missing that we numbered only half of the 70 men who had crossed the river in November.

Our guards were Canadian militiamen who were lodged in a house across the street, some 40 yards away. Four guard posts with sentry boxes surrounded the jail. Supervision seemed slack; usually we were left alone except for a daily visit by the guards' commander, Captain Prentiss, and by those who brought us food twice a day. When weather permitted we were turned out for exercise in a courtyard surrounded by a 20-foot wall.

We knew little of what was happening. Occasionally we heard cannon shots. But whether Arnold had been reinforced and whether he could continue the siege much longer were matters out of our ken. Eventually the winter would end. The river ice would break up and British ships could bring more troops to the city. If Arnold meant to make another try for Quebec he had better do it soon. And if he didn't, what would happen to us?

All in all, it was no wonder that after we came to Dauphin jail we began to make plans for a breakout. The place seemed strong, but we learned, among other things, that some of the iron bars at the windows were corroded where they fitted into the thick stones and could be pried out. Also, after breaking the padlock on a small storage room at the head of the stairs, by a stroke of luck we found a lot of wagon hoops and other pieces of iron which could be made into weapons, and with them a sizable stack of wooden planks.

A committee was formed under the leadership of Sergeant Joseph Ashton, a good engineer of Captain Lamb's artillery company. We went to work on the iron and the planks, bending the hoops flat, sharpening their edges, and binding on notched wooden hilts to make crude swords. The other bits of iron we fashioned as best we could into spearpoints which were set in the ends of split planks.

To hide our weapons we drew the nails out of the top planks of our lower bunks, which were boxlike affairs, cut off the nail heads with a bit of the nail left below them, and put the heads back in the holes to look natural in case of inspection.

According to plan, most prisoners were to escape through the cellar door to the street. The door, which swung inward, was hung from two H-hinges and secured by hasps and a padlock. The hinges and lock were on the inside. It would be no problem to remove them. There was, however, a sentry box 20 feet outside the door. The operation would have to be done quietly and quickly.

A foot of ice against the door on the floor of the cellar was a serious matter. It came from the overflow of a fountain which in warm weather supplied the jail with water. Some of the ice would have to be scraped away so that we could bring the door down inside the cellar and pass out quickly over it.

The operation was well organized. A hundred and fifty men under Ashton were to break out from the door and speed to the St. John's Gate to overwhelm the 30 regulars which observation had shown were posted there. At the same instant others were to jump from the windows and dash for the guardhouse across the street, knock out the guards, and seize their muskets. A smaller group would go for the sentry boxes around the jail, where, in the early morning hour, the sentries would have taken shelter from the cold.

The committee selected March 31 at 3 A.M. as the time for escape, but kept this, as they thought, a secret. Certain men would softly scrape, working two at a time in relays, at the ice with knives until they had cleared it out some inches back of the door. The hinges and lock would be taken off an instant before the breakout. The plan seemed foolproof.

Yet what happened bore out the truth of the saying that even the best-laid scheme can go astray through careless, well-intentioned interference by numbskulls. Two young musketmen, who were not in the inner circle of the plot but who must have overheard something, slipped down into the cellar shortly before the scraping of ice was to begin and started hacking enthusiastically at it with two hatchets we had concealed. Their mental processes were a mystery, but the noise they made was, of course, overheard by the nearest sentry, who gave the alarm.

The leaders quickly decided to plead ignorance of any plan for mass escape, leaving the two dunces to take the penalty for their stupidity. They also agreed to kill anyone who tried to betray the plan—and made sure the decision was generally known.

At dawn we were ordered from our bunks to stand inspection by a major, Captain Prentiss and a file of militia. Ashton and other leaders stuck to their story. They were so convincing that the officers concluded the affair had been an independent effort by two musketmen. They were on the point of leaving when an Englishman who had deserted at Boston and joined our army suddenly leaped from our ranks and took shelter behind the Major. "They're lying, sir," he shrilled. "Protect me and I'll tell you everything."

That afternoon two of the carriages called carioles and three carts came to the entrance of the jail. Out of the carioles stepped General Carleton, two other British officers, and, to my horror, the last man in the world I wanted to face, Hawknose of the cold gray eyes. The carts were loaded with handcuffs and foot shackles attached to heavy iron bars. Under Carleton's supervision, a blacksmith began his job on our company.

There was no place to hide. We were lined up beside

our bunks. With cool assurance our captors watched as one by one we were put in irons. The blacksmith reached the man next to me. Unwillingly my eyes met those of my enemy.

His stare seemed at first blankly impersonal, and my hopes rose. After all, he had seen me only once, or at most twice, and perhaps my appearance had changed. But as he continued to stare his eyes grew more intent. Something about him told me he was suppressing an astonishment such as one feels who thinks he is seeing a ghost.

Abruptly he turned to Carleton and, nodding in my direction, muttered something in a low voice. Carleton's gaze fastened upon me. He said nothing. Hawknose again spoke, urgently. Carleton raised his eyebrows slightly and shook his head. "Highly irregular," he said. "He's a prisoner of war and will be treated as such."

The other continued to argue. The blacksmith had finished handcuffing me and was shackling my left leg to an iron bar.

"No," said Carleton decisively. "He's secure enough, poor devil." Silently I blessed him.

As soon as the British left I told the four who knew of the spies who the man with Carleton was, for none of them had ever seen him.

"We've got to get out of here, in spite of the fix we're in," exclaimed Jerry. "He'll get around Carleton somehow."

"We've all got to get out of here," said Caleb. "But first we must shed these irons if there's any way to do it."

The prisoners began on the job the next day. For a time it seemed hopeless, but at last a few men with small, supple hands, by painfully compressing their palms, squeezed out of their handcuffs. These went to work notching our crude swords with files to make saws, and then began sawing off the rivets of our bonds. Laboriously the rivet heads were detached and false rivets were made from bits of iron. These were ingeniously fashioned to look secure but actually were easy to remove. Thus all but a few whose leg irons were too massive to cope with were able to slip their bonds at night and put them back on in the morning when the guards made their rounds.

Early in the spring scurvy began to appear, the result chiefly of our poor diet. The disease, accompanied by swelling of the gums and other well-known symptoms, became general. Many were taken with such lassitude that they seldom left their bunks.

I had often thought of my family and home, but never more than now. As through a haze I could see my father, tall and weatherbeaten, and hear his soft voice saying, "Take care of yourself, son." And my mother, who had not wanted me to enlist, her kindly face taut at the leave-taking. My younger sister Caroline, who had wept and clung to me like a limpet as we began the march. Would I ever see them again? We grew morose and hopeless. It was the low point of our captivity.

Later, we of Morgan's company were freed of our shackles for some unknown reason and allowed time in the courtyard, where we weakly tried to build up strength by walking hard and playing games. In view of later events it was well that we did.

April passed. Daylight grew rapidly longer. The land became a quagmire from the melting of huge snowdrifts and the showers of spring. On May 1 there was a short snowstorm, winter's last counterattack against the advancing sun.

A few days later we heard the boom of cannon and the pealing of church bells. They saluted the arrival of two British ships which had been waiting in the unfrozen salt water of the lower river for a breakup of ice around the Isle of Orleans. A regiment of soldiers disembarked. The new troops, joined by the garrison, quickly sallied from the gates and fell upon the remaining colonials. The outnumbered Americans fled up the St. Lawrence. The siege of Quebec was over.

From one of the captured Americans we heard the happenings of the winter. Despite his wound, Arnold had been determined to take the city. Congress had promoted him to brigadier general but hadn't helped much otherwise. By the end of March he had recovered sufficiently to mount a horse, which promptly stumbled and fell, crushing his wounded knee.

So Arnold had been forced to give over command to old General Wooster, in charge at Montreal. Our informant said Wooster "hadn't much notion of what to do and had bumbled around a month not doing it." Recently he had been succeeded by General John Thomas, who had brought 500 reinforcements. After seeing Quebec's strength and hearing of the British troops waiting for the ice to break, Thomas had decided the siege was hopeless. He had started to retreat when the British had scattered his men. Carleton ordered all prisoners freed from irons.

About a week later the prisoners were in the court-yard at the time for afternoon exercise. We had been in the place for some time, for it was nearing dusk, when a figure in the uniform of the Canadian militia guards, carrying a musket under his arm, came through the gate and strolled with seeming aimlessness among us. Soon he passed close beside me. "Dave," he murmured.

A quick look at him and my face froze into immobility. He was Jean Claude Merault!

He spoke softly. "Get together your friends. Not more than five or six or we risk failure." He continued on his aimless way.

Quietly I sought out Jerry, Caleb, Solomon, and Bill. I told them to join me one by one at a place I indicated against the face of the wall. They did so, careful not to arouse curiosity among the prisoners. After a time Jean Claude circled back and paused as if to look us over. He spoke in a whisper.

"It will soon be between the dog and the wolf, as we Canadians say, between day and night—what you call twilight. Before that the prisoners must re-enter the jaïl. You five will linger. Make sure all others go before you. Be ready to run with the greatest of quickness to the gate. You understand?"

One might suppose the sudden prospect of escape would have been exciting enough to make us betray ourselves by some sign, but we didn't. Caleb nodded. Solomon spat. Jerry's eyes narrowed slightly. To my surprise I was thinking ahead quite coolly.

"We must stick together getting out," I murmured to Jean Claude. "But if anything happens to separate us, what then?"

"Indeed, what then?"

Inspiration dictated the answer. "If so, we must make our separate ways to the house of our friend Bruiac at Pointe-aux-Trembles within two days if possible. If that is not possible, then we go separately to join Arnold in Montreal."

"Let us hope it will not be necessary."

Jean Claude left us to continue his milling about. In a few minutes the sergeant of the guard, who had been watching the prisoners from his post by the gate, made shoving motions and shouted in broken English that we were to get back to quarters. Slowly, reluctantly, the prisoners obeyed. We five tailed the procession. The sergeant strode to the door of the jail. I wondered how Jean Claude would handle him. He could take at least one shot at us before we got to the gate.

As we reached the door Jean Claude, a few feet away, leveled his musket at the sergeant and gave a curt order. The man gaped in astonishment. He started to raise his gun but at the French boy's sharp warning, hesitated, then dropped it. We leaped for the gate. Jean Claude covered for a moment before dashing after us.

Two militiamen at the gate were momentarily stupefied at the sight of several prisoners followed by a guard running past them, but they reacted quickly to the sergeant's yell. They fired wildly at us and called an alarm to their companions in the guardhouse. With Jean Claude leading, we raced around a corner and turned toward the center of the upper town.

Behind us a hubbub of shouting was punctuated by a few shots. We pounded on around another corner. Suddenly Jean Claude stopped. "We are near the Palace Gate," he gasped. "You must walk ahead of me, as if a prisoner detail, until we see how things are."

Cautiously, watchfully, we came to a row of houses adjacent to the wall. At the corner of the last house Jean Claude peered through the growing twilight. Turning, he whispered: "A sentry is standing in the main arch of the gate. I will divert his attention so he will be looking in the direction away from you. You must quickly creep up behind him and jump him. Time it right; I cannot give you a signal."

Jean Claude strolled toward the guard. We could see him engage the guard in animated talk. He pointed to something down the slope of the cliff. The guard turned his back to us. He looked in the direction Jean Claude indicated.

Swiftly we tiptoed up behind the fellow until we were in leaping distance. I sprang, throwing all the weight of my body on the guard's back. Jerry struck him an instant later. He was hurled to the stone pavement. His gun struck the pavement beside him. With almost a single movement Jerry swooped, retrieved the musket, and swung its butt against the sentry's head. He had no chance to make an outcry.

"C'est bon," said Jean Claude. "Now we descend."

A few steps and we were out of Fortress Quebec.

But we were not out of trouble.

We had passed La Friponne and were keeping to the road through St. Roque when a British patrol marched smartly out of a side street and headed straight for us. We scurried behind the wreckage of some houses, but the British had seen us, or at least had sensed movement.

"Halt," ordered a voice. "Come out, whoever ye are."

We crouched silently, knowing it was too late for accurate shooting and hoping that the patrol would go on toward the battlements above. The officer in command, however, had a different idea. We heard his order to fix bayonets. We heard the rattle of metal rings on musket muzzles. We heard his voice: "Now rout 'em out, lads."

We scattered and ran—ran as fast as our legs could carry us.

12

ENEMY COUNTRY

After a few minutes I stopped to listen and heard the pad of running feet. I tensed, ready to start again.

"That you, Dave?" panted a voice. "Lord, man, ye can bolt like a deer." Jerry halted, breathing hard. A moment later Jean Claude caught up.

"Where are the rest?" I asked him.

"I think they went in the other direction, toward the St. Charles. They were on the opposite side of the road."

Jerry groaned. "Reckon they got caught?"

"Possibly, but I do not think so. They may have run down to the river and found a boat, or they may have circled and made for the hospital. If so, they should rejoin us soon."

"Let's wait a while and see."

But after a half hour Jean Claude grew restive. "Your plan was that if we became separated we would meet at Pointe-aux-Trembles," he reminded me. "But it is late and the nights are short. If we are to reach there at dawn we must march the most rapidly."

Reluctantly I conceded his point. If they had taken to the river we could wait here in vain all night.

Trusting to darkness for protection, we slogged on, making what speed we could on the muddy road, which we left for squishy meadows to avoid the village of St. Foy. When we were safely past the town a sort of delayed emotional reaction took possession of the two ex-prisoners. Jerry and I were free men, by Jemminy! I gleefully imagined the enraged face of Hawknose when he heard the news. We soared on the wings of confidence.

Jean Claude was amused by our mood. He pointed out that it was well to be logical. We were not yet out of the woods, so to speak. We badly needed a change of clothing lest we be spotted by daylight, and we needed food. "There is a place I know of," he added mysteriously. "We shall see when we get there."

It was needful to save our wind for walking, yet Ben and a number of other matters were on my mind, and I had to know the answers. Jean Claude reassured me as to Ben's escape. He had been guided out of town on the night selected. He had made his way safely to the American camp. Next, we asked Jean Claude how he had become a militiaman and had managed today to be at the right place at the right time.

He replied with his usual aplomb that it had been quite simple. He had gone to a recruiting officer soon after Ben's escape and had impressed on the man how much he hated the American *Bostonnais* barbarians. He bore them such ill will that his ambition was to become a guard over them. Then, *tiens,* he would show them they should never dare invade Canada again. "The officer was stupid," he admitted. "But also I was very convincing."

He had been with the guards about ten days when the arrival of the British and the defeat of the Americans, and even more, the resulting letdown in watchfulness, had given him his chance. "And Merault is not such a one as to miss the opportunity," he chuckled. I grinned in the darkness. We had our kind of boasting and he had his. Certainly he had earned the right to preen his feathers.

He told us more of what had been happening in the world while we were cooped up in Quebec. The British had left Boston almost two months ago—back in March. They had simply pulled out and sailed away.

"What happened?" asked Jerry.

"It is said that your General Washington procured heavy guns and mounted them on a high place south of Boston. When the British saw this they knew the game was up."

"That would be Dorchester Heights," I broke in. "Even better than having cannon on Bunker Hill. A short shot right into town. Where did he get the guns?"

"There is a report from Americans who came from Lake Champlain that in the winter a young artillery officer—a fattish man with a harsh name, Knox, I think it was—came to Ticonderoga with many horses and oxen and hauled away many big guns and cannon balls to Albany and then to Boston. If he did that, it was a great feat. The distance must be nearly 300 miles, and over icy roads."

"Think of that," commented Jerry reverently.

Quickening our pace, we stopped talking. Some time later we came to a driveway between two rows of trees. At the end of the drive stood a small unoccupied manor house. We got in by breaking a window. After much groping in the dark we found a candle on a small table. Jean Claude lighted it with his flint.

The place seemed unpromising as we tramped through the almost bare rooms. But by our flickering light we found a large cupboard in which were some old clothes. They were not very good fits but would serve as disguises. Further investigation in the cellar storeroom disclosed a pile of turnips, two good cheeses, and a bag of rather moldy biscuits. We ate hastily and Jerry and I changed into the old clothes. Taking the biscuits and the cheeses, we set off.

Dawn caught us a mile short of Pointe-aux-Trembles. Jean Claude was determined to go on to Bruiac's house alone to scout the situation. He left us in a dense grove of pines near the village.

It was the beginning of a bright May day, still cold and not unlike a day in late March in our more southerly region. We lay drowsily on a mat of pine needles while the light grew stronger and the sun rose. Birds filled the air with chirps, twitters, and whistles. Glowing shafts of sunlight illumined the aisles between the trunks of trees. Puffballs of clouds lazed in the blue sky. It was hard to keep from striding out into the bright day. But our impatience was dampened toward noon when we saw a few ragged American prisoners pass on the road to Quebec under guard of Canadian militiamen.

Jean Claude returned with our gnarled little friend Bruiac, who carried a sack containing bread, baked potatoes, and a roasted fowl. He was friendly but worried. He feared both for us and for his family if he gave us refuge. When the Americans seemed to be winning, the peasants were well disposed, but now that they had seen our men pouring through town in retreat, and had suffered from looting, their faces were turned against us. They expected the British to come soon from Quebec.

Bruiac, however, had a plan. We must spend the rest of the day in hiding. He had sent his oldest son with a message to a cousin who lived on a secluded farm to the west, away from the river. We would stay at the cousin's farm until we found a way to get to Montreal. Tonight he would guide us there.

"What about Caleb, Solomon and Bill?" I objected.

Jean Claude shrugged. "We hope they will appear but we have no assurance of it. If they do, Bruiac will take care of them. Otherwise, they must find their way themselves."

The month and more that we spent with the cousin, François Laborde, his wife Celeste, and their five small bright-eyed children was a time of frustration and unexpected trouble. We were not welcome. We were regarded as a dangerous burden laid on them for some inexplicable reason, to be got rid of as soon as possible. We, in turn, were eager to be on our way. Jean Claude soon went to the nearest village. On his return he informed us that the British had not yet advanced from Quebec but that the rearguard of our army was now far up the river. If we left, we must keep to back country, traveling at night. The alternative would be to await developments.

The decision was made for us. Jerry fell ill of a fever. This may have been the delayed result of privations during the winter, or it may have been caused by exhalations from the damp ground after the snow melted, which some people held to be in the nature of a miasma, with bad effects on the body. I know nothing of such matters but was inclined to doubt the miasma theory, as I had never experienced anything like that in spring.

May passed into June as Jerry slowly recovered and began to regain strength. Jean Claude had been away for a week when he returned with news that more British had arrived at Quebec under a General John Burgoyne, who was said to be a favorite of King George—Gentleman Johnny, his soldiers called him. With the British had come regiments of Germans from the principality of Brunswick, hired by the King to fight Americans. These were led by a Baron Riedesel. Morgan's riflemen later were to have conclusive dealings with both of these gentlemen.

Against the British reinforcements, Jean Claude continued, we had done some reinforcing ourselves. A brigade of well-trained, handsomely equipped Americans from the middle colonies had recently come down Lake Champlain and reached Sorel, where the Richelieu joins the St. Lawrence. They were commanded by a General Sullivan and they aimed at nothing less than taking Quebec.

It sounded well, yet I had doubts about it.

"How far's this Sorel from here?" demanded Jerry eagerly.

Jean Claude considered. "About a hundred miles. But if the Americans advance, we might meet them nearer, perhaps at Three Rivers."

"Then what's keepin' us?"

Although Jerry was grimly determined, we had to stop every few hours to let him rest, so progress was slow. Avoiding villages and enemy patrols, we reached Three Rivers at last and walked boldly into town, expecting it to be occupied by Americans.

But now came another of the bitter disappointments that had been our lot since we entered Canada. The impetuous Sullivan had sent a subordinate with 2,000 men from Sorel to attack Three Rivers. They had landed above the place at night, had floundered through swamps, and when they got there found a British fleet and many troops awaiting them. They had fought bravely but had been thrown back and cut to pieces. The survivors had retreated to Sorel. Carleton's vanguard, led by Burgoyne, had followed them.

We plodded through forests and meadows for six days. At Berthier, some 50 miles from Montreal, we heard that Arnold's garrison had left Montreal in the middle of June for St. Johns on the Richelieu to join Sullivan and the remains of other commands. A little later, all of them, carrying their sick and wounded, had retreated up the Richelieu. The British held Sorel, on the south bank of the St. Lawrence not far from here. Now we had no choice but to go to Montreal. There we would cross the river and strike toward the New York wilderness through country we didn't know, amid imagined perils all the greater because of our ignorance. At Berthier, Jean Claude bought civilian clothes and discarded his uniform.

At dusk five days later we reached Montreal. The houses stood along the river and inland the town was dominated by the looming hump of Mont Royale. We passed the ramparts and came to Chateau Ramesay, a steep-roofed stone building which had been the American headquarters. It was separated from the street by a fence, and a British sentry stood at its door. Above the town rose the towers of the Sulpicians and the spires of three other churches. There were other buildings that appeared to be convents. In the gathering darkness we passed along a narrow street lined with small houses until we came to an inn, where we were received without question.

Next morning, on the road to Lachine, where we would cross the river, I was wondering what Jean Claude intended to do now that we were on our way out of Canada. At length I asked him.

"I can do little here." He shrugged. "The only hope for a free Canada is for your colonies to win the war. Then perhaps—" He broke off moodily, but soon added: "I will go with you wherever that takes me. Some day I will come back."

I grasped his hand. "Good. We'll stick together."

At Lachine we found a boatman who agreed to row us across the river to an Indian village called Caughnawaga, where we bought some jerked venison for the trip.

The date was July 11th. To the best of my reckoning we were well over 100 miles as a bird flies, and much more as a man walks, from the first place we could be sure of rejoining the army, which would be Crown Point or Ticonderoga. Taking off in a southeasterly direction toward where we supposed the lower end of Lake Champlain to be, we went on until dark making good speed, until we stopped for the night.

The first sign of danger was a running buck that flashed past us, white tail bobbing with each leap. The deer had been frightened by something ahead of us. He was gone in an instant.

Jerry frowned. We studied the woods carefully. It was just past noon of an oppressively hot day. "What is it?" asked Jean Claude. I motioned for silence. I wished I had a gun. Our only weapons were Jean Claude's musket and Jerry's knife. After a moment we cautiously advanced. Then it happened.

An Indian jumped from behind a tree, his musket leveled at me. Jean Claude shouted. I whirled to see him struggling with two savages. Two others seized Jerry. A hard arm around my neck choked off breath. Quickly our arms were bound behind our backs.

They were big, horrible-looking Indians. Their blackened faces were daubed with scowling patterns of vermilion and ochre and their scalp locks stood stiffly above the shaven sides of their heads. They were like creatures in a nightmare.

A man in the green buckskins of a Canadian Ranger stepped from a clump of bushes. He was short and wiry, with a lean brown face. After a moment he spoke to the Indians in a guttural language. Roughly we were prodded into motion. With the Canadian leading and the savages bunched around us, we set off at a rapid pace, which continued through the long afternoon without letup. The Indians were tireless as wolves. About two hours before sundown we met some Canadian militia, who exchanged words with the Ranger.

Soon we reached a road and passed some cleared ground. We could see, across the flatland bordering a river, a cluster of buildings and smaller dwellings. In the midst of the village were two earthwork ramparts, fraised with protective stakes, surrounding several structures and connected by a palisaded passageway.

"St. Johns," exclaimed Jean Claude.

Drawing nearer we perceived that the town had suffered a good deal from Montgomery's siege in the fall of '75 and during the recent American evacuation. A number of houses had been burned; others were empty and boarded up. Innumerable horses and oxen grazed the meadows on both sides of the Richelieu. Artillery and carts were parked in the fields.

St. Johns was filled with British soldiers. In spite of the heat they wore regulation tight scarlet coats, pipe-clayed white breeches, and, around their necks, uncomfortable leather stocks. There were other troops in long blue coats with silver facings, and leather breeches. These I took to be the German mercenaries.

Some had tall hats that must have weighed pounds apiece and some, in cumbersome jackboots, were dragoons.

If we were intent on sizing up our enemies they were no less curious about us and our Indian captors. By the time we reached the bastions overlooking the river we were surrounded and trailed by idle Redcoats. Some were actively hostile. One, who appeared to have been tipping the rum pot too often, cursed us for rebel scum. His toadies joined in the blackguarding. Thus encouraged, the drunken one aimed a blow at me which missed but struck an Indian on the shoulder. The savage whirled on him, tomahawk raised. The Ranger gobbled something and the Indian sullenly lowered his weapon. A thickset figure in buckskins suddenly plowed through the crowd. "Get back, you," he growled. "Make room."

"Capitaine Barwick!" cried the Ranger in relief.

"All right, Jouet. Prisoners, eh? Good."

The voice stirred a memory—a memory that quickly became an anguished certainty. The face of the man beside the Ranger was roundish, clean-shaven, and there was a scar on the left cheek. Once more I confronted the man who on the bank of the Kennebec had ordered his Indians to kill me.

As he stared at me his insolent expression changed. His eyes, once so falsely affable, narrowed. He looked intently at Jerry. His lips twisted into a leering smile. "Well, well, well," he fairly purred. "The bad penny turns up again. And one of his pals with him. Tremaine will enjoy this."

Tremaine! So this man's companion had kept the

name he had used at Cambridge. And Arnold had insisted that Tremaine was loyal. Again I wondered at this mystery. Was he actually the man Arnold knew?

"To our camp with them, Jouet. Quick."

The Ranger spoke to the Indians, who pressed against the crowd. Glowering, the soldiers resisted. "Stop shoving, you dirty weasels," yelled one. "Let's take 'em away from the savages," cried another. "By jingo, have some fun with them. . . . Make them run the gantlet. . . . Let's go, lads!"

What might have been a bloody clash was suddenly averted by a resonant, authoritative voice.

"Men! Men! Stop this brawling."

At the words every Redcoat froze like a statue.

The speaker was a tall officer in a splendid uniform. His long, silver-frogged blue coat was unbuttoned because of the heat but he wore a high black stock just the same. His commanding eyes, straight nose, and full-fleshed lips over a large round chin gave him an imperious look.

"What is the cause of this unseemly behavior?" he demanded of the one who called himself Barwick.

"General, these prisoners are rebels and spies the Lieutenant and his Indians caught in the woods. Likely they were skulking around waiting to kill a British officer or two."

"Sir, we are not spies or skulkers," I broke in. "We are simply Americans out of uniform who were trying to get back to our army in New York Province. I beg you to treat us as prisoners of war and not leave us in the hands of savages."

The General regarded me haughtily. "Whatever you are, my young hearty, you are fortunate to be captive of His Majesty's invincible forces, commanded here by myself, Lieutenant General John Burgoyne. Your army, as you call it, no longer exists as a fighting force, if it ever did. It is a disorganized mob, starving and diseased."

I started to answer hotly, but thought better of it.

"Here, misguided rebels though you be, victims of a handful of connivers against the King's peace, you will be treated humanely, as will all others who perceive the error of their ways and throw themselves on His Majesty's mercy."

He sounded as if he was speaking in Parliament. Later I learned that he had often done just that. He was a high muck-a-muck, a playwright, a natural actor, and a favorite of George III. A puffed up and vain man was Gentleman Johnny, who looked much younger than his age, which was in the fifties, but he was no fool, for all that later happened to him. In spite of his pontifical ways, he was a rather pleasant man as stuffy British generals go.

Scarface began to protest, saying the Indians were touchy about their honor, hard enough to control anyway. He made quite an argument of it while my heart hung in my throat. But it didn't help him any.

General Burgoyne turned to an aide beside him. "Jermyn, detail six men and take the prisoners to the provost." To the Ranger lieutenant he said: "You speak the tongue of these Indians, I take it. Tell them this."

He launched into another discourse, calling the savages "brave, noble brothers" whose warlike feats were known to all and whose help was much cherished by "the Great Father across the sea." He fed them more of this talk while the Indians began to strut and howl. But as we left, the tenor of his remarks changed. He reminded them of strict orders that prisoners were not to be mistreated, and that scalps were to be taken only from the dead, never from women or children or the wounded.

What the Indians made of it all I never knew. Probably some of the speech was toned down to lessen its critical effect and parts may have been lost in translation. But whatever Burgoyne next said to his soldiers must have hit the mark, for we heard behind us an outburst of laughter and cheers for Gentleman Johnny. Windbag he might be, but he was popular with his troops.

We were confined on the second floor of what had been a British barracks within one of the two earthworks. There we joined some fifty other American prisoners, sick men and stragglers who had been overtaken when Arnold, Sullivan, and others had left St. Johns on the run.

One of these was a man named Goodhue who had been with Montgomery when he invaded Canada. I asked him if he remembered a tall, thin-faced, hawk-nosed officer who had joined Montgomery's army about that time and had called himself Tremaine.

"Of course I do," he replied. "A dirty traitor turncoat. Saw him first at the siege of this place, St. Johns, that held us up for weeks. A lot of things went wrong then and I'll wager this fellow, who was acting as an aide to Montgomery, had much to do with it. Why are you asking about him?" he added suspiciously.

I told him as much of my story as I thought necessary, and said that I was worried by the fact that Tremaine's helper had recognized me here.

"Don't wonder you are," he said thoughtfully. "Your man rode high and handsome for a time. Then I heard that somebody who knew the real Tremaine turned up and denounced him as an impostor. Anyway, he disappeared. Next thing was found out, he'd joined that French devil La Corne St. Luc and his murdering Indians."

I had heard of St. Luc from some of Lamb's men in Quebec. Serving the British, he had used western Indians ruthlessly as killers of frontier settlers.

After the fall of Montreal to Montgomery, Goodhue had remained there with the small garrison and had heard nothing more of the turncoat.

"He was in Quebec with Carleton," I explained. "He tried to persuade Carleton to turn me over to him."

"Then it's mighty lucky Burgoyne happened to save you here," he exclaimed.

Constantly in our ears was a tapping and thwacking from a small shipyard on the river bank which we could see from a window in the barrack. The British were putting together a fleet to sail up Lake Champlain. We learned from a guard that some of the smaller craft were being constructed from numbered parts made in England. The ribs of the largest vessel gave the impression that it might become a sloop of war or a frigate. Another was shaping into a schooner, and there was a big cumbersome thing meant to carry a lot of heavy guns. There were also some gunboats.

The hot summer days dragged on interminably through the remainder of July and all of August. We were caged. But we thought always of how to escape and rejoin our people.

Our captors themselves eventually provided a way. In September, evidently worried by the time it was taking to build the fleet, they began sending prisoners under guard to help by carrying timbers, cordage, and ammunition for the carpenters and riggers. We three observed matters carefully. We noted that the guards, whether from overconfidence or boredom, were getting slack. Jerry had spotted a canoe, which no one seemed to bother about, tied to the stern of a gunboat. A good deal of time passed, however, before we could do anything about it.

By the third week of September the fleet was virtually completed and we were almost in despair, for we knew that very soon our services would be dispensed with and our chance lost. Then, late one afternoon, when our guard had turned his back and walked away to chat with a friend, we jumped aboard a gunboat and hid ourselves under a spare sail which we had carried into the hold earlier that day.

Thanks to luck and British carelessness, we were not discovered. As soon as night came we emerged, helped ourselves to some beef and ship's biscuits, found paddles, crept to the canoe, untied it—and were off.

All night we paddled up the Richelieu, passing an island I judged to be Isle aux Noix, and by dawn were near the outlet of Champlain. We went ashore, hid ourselves and the canoe in the woods, and took turns sleeping and standing guard. The next night we entered the lake, keeping close to its western shore. Five days later, after a delay caused by a high wind that made canoeing dangerous, we came to Ticonderoga.

The fort stood above a narrow point of the lake, which, pinched in by heights, was here barely a quarter of a mile wide. The site was a peninsula between the narrows and a river which was the outlet of Lake George, to the southwest. Thus it commanded both waterways, denying them to an enemy. Its disadvantage was that it lay under three heights, one directly across the narrows to the east, another across the Lake George outlet, and a third back of the fort. If an enemy got possession of these it might be fatal.

We landed at a low point of land jutting into the lake. On it, emplaced in a fortification, were a number of good-sized cannon. On higher ground back of this stood the bluish-gray stone barracks, redoubts, magazines, and formidable guns of Ticonderoga. A bridge near the point connected the east shore with the fort. An odd-looking vessel was moored to a dock near the shore redoubt. As we watched, a cannon from a row along the dock was slowly hoisted by block and tackle and swung aboard.

After telling our story to an officer at the shore battery, we learned from him what had been happening during our imprisonment. General Horatio Gates, last seen by me at Washington's headquarters, was in command of the Champlain area, under General Schuyler, the northern commander, and had been since June. The officer admired him, saying that he had restored discipline among the survivors of Canada, had collected fresh troops and had greatly strengthened the fort.

The summer had been a busy one for all, he continued. Especially for Benedict Arnold. Because of Arnold's seafaring experience Gates had given him free rein to build and arm a sort of navy on this inland waterway. It was a crucial move; the enemy, facing 100 miles of wilderness, would have to transport themselves and their supplies by water. They must be stopped on the lake.

Ship carpenters from the seaboard had been recruited at high pay. They had come to Skenesborough at the southern end of the lake, where there was a sawmill, and, driven by Arnold's energy, had built a number of sail vessels, the last of which they were now finishing. Arnold was down the lake with a small fleet, watching for the British. (I wondered why we had not sighted him; perhaps he had passed on the day we didn't dare to brave the lake.)

When we described what we had seen of the shipbuilding at St. Johns and told him that the British must now be on the way, he said that we should tell General Gates; he would have an orderly fetch Captain Wilkinson, the General's aide.

Young Captain Wilkinson greeted us with an air of

vast portentousness, which we learned was his cus-
tomary manner, whether the matter was of any conse-
quence or not. He conducted us up to the fort, through
the gate, and thence to the General's office.

Gates peered at us over his glasses, looking more
than ever like an aging schoolmaster. When I told him
we had just come from Canada, he said in a petulant
but not unkindly manner, "Yes, yes, but you must be
brief."

I described what we had seen of the shipbuilding at
St. Johns.

"General Arnold will have his work cut out for him,
but he will manage," he commented. He adjusted his
spectacles and looked hard at me. "I have seen you
somewhere before."

I reminded him of the scene in Washington's headquarters when I had charged that the man calling himself Tremaine was a spy, and told him I had again
fallen afoul of the man and his helper at Quebec and
St. Johns.

"My, my," he commented. "Now I recall it, I thought
the whole thing very odd. When we come to grips we
must watch out for this fellow." He began to shuffle the
papers on his desk. Then he had a new thought.
"Wilkinson, my dear fellow, we must get these men
into decent uniforms, will you see to it?" He nodded
vigorously, which would have amused Morgan. We left
somewhat puzzled. He was a capable general no doubt,
but he seemed to us a fussbudget.

On our second day at Ticonderoga two more of the
odd-looking boats, rowed awkwardly by green crews,

appeared from the south and anchored at the dock.
Riggers began stepping two short masts in each and
soldiers started hoisting cannon aboard.

Idly watching, I saw a familiar figure drop from one
of the boats to the dock. I stared, scarce believing my
eyes. "Caleb!" I yelled. "Caleb!"

He stared an instant, bawled, "Jumping Jerusalem!"
and came on the run.

Joyously we threw our arms around him, laughing,
pounding him on the back with our fists. Jerry kept
repeating, "You old son of a gun, you." Jean Claude
lapsed into rapid-fire French. Soldiers at the hoist almost dropped a brass cannon through the bottom of a
boat as they watched in astonishment.

When we could speak connectedly we learned that
Solomon was at Crown Point with other invalids; he
had been ill of a fever. Bill Riddle was at Skenesborough working on the last of the boats. Caleb was
now second in command of a schooner with Arnold's
fleet. He had come up from Skenesborough to bring the
two new boats for outfitting. He said they were row
galleys, adapted from Mediterranean coastal galleys,
rigged with two triangular lateen sails. They were
easily maneuvered and capable of carrying good
armament.

How had he gotten here? What had happened on
that spring evening under Quebec's walls when we had
dashed our separate ways?

He and Solomon and Bill had gained the bank of the
St. Lawrence and hidden in a bateau. Later they had
rowed across the St. Lawrence and escaped by way of

the south shore. They had caught up with the retreating army at St. Johns.

"Now I have a surprise for David," said Caleb with a chuckle. "Remember there was a fellow who got out of Quebec before us?" He strode to the galley and called to someone inside it.

The one who answered jumped to the dock, stood motionless for an instant, then rushed toward me. "Dave!" he cried.

"Ben!" I shouted. "At last."

As we clutched each other's shoulders I was not ashamed of the tear mist that suddenly blurred my sight.

13

BATTLE ON THE LAKE

Valcour Island lies close to the New York shore of Lake Champlain, about 60 miles north of Ticonderoga. Its humpbacked, tree-covered mass is separated from the mainland by a narrow channel, which widens into a bay on the southwest side of the island. Coming at it in mid-lake from the south, it appears to be a peninsula until you see the narrow passage beyond the bay.

As we approached it on this bright, chilly morning of October 6th, it seemed peaceful and deserted, merely another bit of the colorful autumn panorama—flaming foliage of hardwoods and greens of spruce and hemlock—that spread before us on either side. Our big triangular sails were drawing well; the idle rowers shivered in the wind. Snow lay on the crests of the mountains to the east. Alert in the bow of the low-lying galley, Caleb watched our course toward the island.

"Where are them ships you've been talkin' about?" demanded Jerry. "I don't see any."

"Now you're in the navy, even if it's only a

scraped-up raggety one, you ought to use the right words," Caleb told him severely. "Strictly speaking, ships are three-masted full-riggers, and none of these are. Schooners are two-masted fore-and-aft rigged. Sloops of war can be rigged different ways. What we've got here are four lateen-rigged row galleys, counting the small one, two sloops, two schooners, and eight gundelos—sixteen vessels with maybe ninety guns, near all of them twelve-pounders or less. Kind of light-weight, but we'll see."

"I still don't spy any of your floatin' what-you-call 'ems."

"You will in a minute. That's the beauty of it. Arnold's a seaman. He looked all over until he found this spot."

"Perhaps I am stupid," put in Jean Claude. "I do not understand."

Caleb explained that the British would probably wait for a favorable north wind to come up the lake from the Richelieu. Our fleet would be hidden behind the island until the enemy passed it. Then we would show ourselves and the British would have to beat back against the wind to fight us. We would have an advantage. And the British would have to fight; if they left us behind them we could destroy their army on the lake. Arnold's real aim was to delay the invasion until winter made it impossible. If he could do this, the colonies would gain months of valuable time. Already, merely by building this fleet, he had made the British, who knew of it, lose several weeks in strengthening their own.

This sounded ominous, as if Arnold was willing to sacrifice his own fleet to upset enemy plans. "Are they much stronger than we are?" I asked.

"Well, I wouldn't say that. A little maybe."

The words were scarce out of Caleb's mouth when puffballs of white smoke bloomed ahead of us and we heard the boom of saluting guns. Now I could make out masts and furled sails above a thicket of greenery. The fleet was drawn up in a crescent near to shore across the bay on this side of the island. It had seemed part of the forest behind it because evergreen branches were lashed to the vessels' bulwarks to disguise them.

Caleb barked an order. Our speed slackened and we glided gracefully into the line of vessels whose crews cheered us wildly, welcoming the final addition to the American flotilla.

Our two sails were quickly clewed to their spars and we came to anchor close to the *Trumbull* galley, with the *Congress* on the other side. Next in line was the schooner *Royal Savage*, which had been captured from the British in the Canadian invasion, and beyond it was the schooner *Revenge*. Arnold, neat as always, in blue and buff, came aboard with the captain who was to command the galley. The General's protuberant, darting eyes took in everything. He complimented Caleb on his seamanship, ordered the new captain to fasten hemlock boughs to the bulwarks, and was off to inspect other craft.

Caleb, who was the lieutenant of the *Revenge*, had told us he would take all four of us with him if we wished, as the *Revenge* was undermanned. Ben and

Jerry and I could act as marines, shooting at the crews of attacking vessels, and Jean Claude could help the cannoneers. So we transferred to the schooner, whose captain, fittingly enough, was named Seaman.

Next day the wind was variable and weak. It swung to the south again and held there for two more days. The *Revenge* was assigned to watch duty. Each morning we rounded the point of Valcour and sailed up the wide channel between it and Grand Isle, looking for the British. Each afternoon we beat back on long tacks to report to Arnold. It was futile work, but it was necessary even though we didn't expect the British until the wind changed.

On the morning of October 11th, however, things were different. Late the day before, the wind had swung around to the northeast, cold and cutting, kicking up an endless succession of whitecaps on the lake. The sloop *Liberty* was sent back to Ticonderoga for supplies, reducing the fleet to fifteen. As we left the anchorage, all aboard were alert and expectant. Arnold had ordered us to run back the moment we sighted the enemy. Rounding the point of Valcour, we could see snow on the Adirondack Mountains to the west as well as on the summits to the east. We sailed close to the wind toward Grand Isle. The streaked water was blue under the bright sun and the cold made our teeth chatter.

The *Revenge* had tacked once and was nearing the end of its second leg when Caleb, who was watching from a perch on the mainmast, called down: "Here they are! Rounding a point about six miles north.

One full-rigger—looks like a big sloop of war—and two schooners. Calculate the schooners are sixteen-gunners." He slid down the mast like a monkey. The *Revenge* came about, racing for the tip of the island.

Rounding the point we fired a gun, and as we reached in to closer quarters Captain Seaman bawled his news to Arnold. We turned again to watch the British. Instantly there was great activity in the little fleet. Looking back, we saw boats putting off from the various craft. Arnold was calling a council of captains.

When at last the British came in full view past the point we were awed by their strength. Into the broad reach of lake south of the island sailed the big sloop of war and the two schooners we had first sighted. Behind them were two smaller sloops. Next came a craft with a towering height of sail—the barge we had seen under construction at St. Johns. It was awkward-looking but it was a formidable gun platform, low in the water from its weight of heavy artillery. Surrounding it was a veritable fleet of gunboats and gundelos, most of them larger than any of ours. Following these were many bateaux carrying troops, and big master canoes crammed with Indians. It was a grand display of power.

The leading British vessels were well out in the lake to the south when sails blossomed on our *Royal Savage* and the row galleys as they left the battle crescent. We turned back into the bay. Gathering speed, the American vessels headed out into the lake. Arnold was following his plan to make the British come into the bay against the wind where their necessary maneuverings might enable him to fight them piecemeal. It also seemed that he intended to take a slap at the enemy gunboats, which were now beginning to round the point into the bay.

From our regained place in the line we had a good view of the efforts that the British, having sighted the *Royal Savage* and the galleys, were making to beat back into the bay. One schooner was scoring progress with short tacks. The less maneuverable square-rigger was having more difficulty, and so was the other schooner. The sloops and the cumbersome gun platform were not in sight.

The galleys and our schooner exchanged some shots with the gunboats, then started firing at long range at the schooner. Its guns thudded in answer. After a while the Americans turned back toward their anchorage. Half a mile offshore the galleys clewed up their sails, took to oars, and were soon in their places. The *Royal Savage*, close-hauled, aimed for its anchorage but lacking oars, had trouble. It ran out on a tack and came about to the east for another. The well-handled British sloop of war changed course and began to overtake it. Anxiously we watched the contest.

"Stretching it too far," muttered Caleb as the *Royal Savage* kept on a course toward the tip of the island. "Come about, man, come about," he pleaded softly.

He was right. Suddenly the *Royal Savage* hit bottom in a shallow and canted a bit on its side before sails could be lowered. There it lay, off to the east of the battle line, as the British ship worked up to within range. Watchers groaned. Captain Seaman yelled an

order to double-shot the guns and he and Caleb jumped around, laying them on the target for the inexperienced crew.

Our guns went off in a ragged volley. A moment later the British full-rigger raked the *Royal Savage* with its heavy, long-range guns in a rippling flash of fire that stabbed through the billows of white smoke. Our anchored fleet joined the fight in an incredible din of explosions. Canted though it was, the *Royal Savage* replied to the British vessel, though not very effectively, for half the crew were trying to get it afloat again. I could see them doing something with a boat and a cable.

The range was too great for rifle fire. We three laid down our weapons and, putting on the rope harness

used for the purpose, helped the cannoneers haul back our 12-pounders for swabbing and reloading after each discharge. Above us the two masts of the schooner stood stark, bare of sail.

Amid the haze of smoke I saw some of the enemy gunboats, with one big gun in each bow, coming in like beetles to pound the stranded schooner. Others pulled closer to engage our gundelos, most of which lay between the *Royal Savage* and the *Revenge.* Figures of men, small in the distance, jumped from the deck of the *Savage* and swam toward the shore of the island. The square-rigger, still battling the wind, turned its attention from the *Royal Savage* and tried a few long shots from its heaviest guns, but the balls fell short.

Meanwhile, the nearest British schooner had tacked.

With sails filled, it was on a course bringing it across our front. It gave us a broadside as it passed, fired another at the *Congress* and was near the center of our line when something happened. Perhaps the wind, uncertain in the sheltered bay, suddenly changed; at any rate the schooner swung around heading straight for the galleys, then fell off and stood almost motionless, its sails fluttering.

The galleys grasped the opportunity. Their fire, which had slackened a bit, was furiously renewed. The *Enterprise* and the *Revenge* joined in, shooting as fast as guns could be reloaded and aimed. The cannonade grew into a great roar of continuous thunderclaps, a cataclysm of sound.

This iron hail took its toll. I could see men aboard the schooner working frantically to get it moving again. Some went down under blasts of grapeshot. I tried several shots at the deck but the distance was long for accuracy. Holes and rips appeared in the sails. Pieces of rigging fell. Splotches and gashes could be seen on the hull where solid shot had penetrated or, bouncing off the stout timbers, had knocked off paint. The schooner had water in the hull; it was listing slightly. We had hurt it; half its guns were silent. But however hard we tried, our ordnance simply was not heavy enough to sink the vessel.

British gunboats now came to the schooner's aid. Their big cannons matched or outmatched anything we had. One of them was hit and set afire. In a few minutes it blew up with a roar and a great mushrooming of smoke. We kept pounding the schooner, though at a slower rate now, for the guns were dangerously hot. Through the heavy veil of smoke I saw the other British schooner slowly coming in to rescue its companion.

The *Royal Savage*'s masts were down. A boat filled with men left the shattered hulk, heading toward us. Two British gunboats now reached their helpless schooner and under a hail of grapeshot began with brave determination to tow it slowly away. Hours—I had no notion how many—had passed since we had sighted the British coming up the lake, but the sun was still fairly high. Three enemy gunboats now concentrated their fire on the *Revenge*.

The boatload from the *Royal Savage* arrived. As the powder-blackened men scrambled aboard amid the thuds of balls against our hull, they gabbled and pointed urgently to the nearby shore of Valcour. There I saw an Indian kneel, fire a musket, and jump behind a tree. British-led savages were ashore on the island! Other muskets flashed. This was a new danger. Ben and Jerry and I went to work, sighting carefully.

We winged several Indians as, minute by minute, the long cannons on the gunboats boomed away, the shots screeching over and around us. I was reloading when something hit me with the force of a horse's kick, spinning me around. The next instant I heard a great *whoosh* above me, a crash, then the cracking of timber. Something struck my head. That was the last I knew of the battle of Valcour Island.

14

INTERLUDE

It was pleasant to sit by the window in my room munching an apple as I idly watched the wind toss the limbs of trees that now, in late March, were still bare of leaves. Birds whistled and chirped as if joyed by the strength of the returning sun. It was good to be alive and looking forward to the quick burgeoning of spring in the Shenandoah.

At the east of the valley the last remains of snow lingered on the crests of the Blue Ridge. The sight reminded me of the early snow on the Adirondacks as we sailed on Champlain watching for the British in that seemingly long-ago time which was actually a little less than six months in the past. It was good to be alive. I had been lucky.

Those memories of the winter . . . they were a mingling of fevered dreams, consciousness of great pain and despair, then the boredom of gradual recovery and impatience to be up and about. In the course of time I had been told by Ben and Jerry what had happened to me in that battle-clamorous afternoon off Valcour

Island and what had befallen Arnold's outgunned little fleet.

The blow I had felt as I stood on the deck of the *Revenge* had been the impact of a musket ball that must have been fired by an Indian on the shore of Valcour. The bullet had hit my chest, had broken a rib, and had buried itself near my left shoulder blade. A moment later a cannon ball from a gunboat had smashed the foremast, bringing down the top of it. This had fallen on me, grazing the back of my head. It had not hit squarely, else my skull, thick though it seems to be, would have been smashed like a gooseberry. As it was, I suffered a serious concussion. Jerry had been momentarily dazed when the ball hit the mast above him. When he told of this he recalled his earlier disdain of British artillery.

"I was plumb ashamed of criticizing 'em," he admitted. "That shot was mighty close. I could hear the angels' wings beatin' as they come for me, though truth to tell I wasn't sure whether they was angels or the folk from the other place. Caleb said most of the gunboats had German cannoneers. Maybe they're better than the British, or maybe not. Anyhow, whoever aimed that gun is an aimer to stay away from."

Arnold's fleet had battled until dark. The *Royal Savage*, set afire by the enemy, had blown up. Getting organized at last, the British had waited for daylight, confident of finishing us. But outwitting them again, and aided by a fog, Arnold had slipped past them in the night. Two days later they caught up with him and he lost more of the fleet. Five vessels, including the

Revenge, finally reached Ticonderoga. Carleton had occupied Crown Point but had decided that it was too late in the season to attack Ticonderoga. On November 3rd he had started his army back to Canada for the winter. Arnold's daring gamble for time had paid off.

I had known nothing of all this while it was happening. Ben told me that I had been unconscious for days after the fight and had wasted to a skeleton for lack of nourishment. With Carleton threatening the fort, the most seriously wounded and sick were sent to Albany by way of Lake George, then overland to Fort Edward on the Hudson, and on by water the rest of the way. It was on the land stretch of this journey that I began to regain wits enough to feel excruciating pain with every jolt of the wagon.

In the hospital more weeks of agony followed. Much of the time my mind was addled. I could not think; I could not remember; yet there were intervals of sense when I feared that my brain had been permanently damaged by the lick on the head. A surgeon extracted the ball from my chest, but the wound refused to heal and I ran high fevers.

During part of this period Ben was with me. After Carleton retreated Ben got leave to come to Albany. I may owe my life to him. He nursed me, made me eat, cheered me, and, perhaps most important of all, kept the doctor from bleeding me too often—which was about all the sawbones could think of to do.

For me, the last of the year 1776 dragged out in this dreary, painful fashion, while my naturally healthy body began to recuperate. Worry about my sanity gradually left me and although the chest wound was far from healed, the time of fever seemed past. Ben had returned to Ticonderoga, where Jean Claude, Caleb, and the others had remained. I began to think eagerly of going home. When Jerry turned up at the hospital in January on furlough for Winchester I judged I had convalesced enough to join him. The doctor didn't argue. He had plenty of other patients to bleed.

We went by boat to Kingston on the Hudson and after a day's delay got a ride in an army supply wagon down almost to the border of Pennsylvania. Begging or hiring rides from farmers, we eventually reached Philadelphia, a fine big place, where Congress was in session. The regular stage coach carried us on to York. We were now on the Great Wagon Road which stretched through Maryland by way of Frederick, on to Winchester, and down the long Valley of Virginia into North Carolina. Slowly we made our way until we sighted the familiar Blue Ridge. We crossed the Potomac, reached Winchester, and soon were home. Even though the time was late in February and everything was covered with snow, home had never looked so good to me.

Now, solicitously cared for by my sister Caroline and stuffing myself with my mother's good cooking, I was in danger of becoming spoiled. Every day I grew stronger in body and mind—so much so that I was beginning to think of the day when I would rejoin the army and start fighting the war again. Right now, however, there wasn't much war to fight.

At about the time we were battling Carleton on

Champlain the main struggle had been around New York. The British had forced Washington's army to withdraw to a place called Westchester, where there had been a battle. The Americans fell back again and Washington lost two forts commanding the Hudson, one of them on Manhattan Island. Slowly the Americans had retreated down through New Jersey and crossed the Delaware into Pennsylvania. In December most of the British had gone into winter quarters in New York, leaving garrisons at several places in New Jersey.

Washington soon struck at one of these—Trenton, occupied by Germans. On the day after Christmas he surprised the garrison and virtually destroyed it. The British responded by sending columns toward Trenton. Washington outfoxed them, flanked them, and at Princeton thrashed them. The British retreated to a base at New Brunswick. Washington and his tired little army set up headquarters at Morristown, New Jersey, where they continued to harry the British until they regained nearly all the Province. They were still there. At last report Ben and Jerry were with them.

One of the first things I had heard in Albany, when I had recovered sufficiently to grasp such matters, was news of Morgan and our Quebec fellow prisoners. After Morgan had spiritedly refused Carleton's offer of a general's commission in the British army, he and the men had been exchanged on parole, back in August. They had been sent by ship to New Jersey and had scattered to their various "states," as the old provinces were now called. I was glad to hear this, but in my low spirit at the time it seemed ironic that we had gone to such trouble to escape when by staying in prison in Quebec we would have been free men a full half month before Valcour.

When I got home I heard that Morgan, warmly praised by Washington, had been commissioned a colonel and ordered to raise a rifle regiment—the 11th Virginia—for the Continental Army. That was a fitting tribute to the big, inspired bear of a leader who on the march to Quebec had been at the same time both loved and hated by the rugged individualists he commanded.

It was odd that, just as I was musing on this and again wondering how long it would be before I could rejoin Big Dan and my friends, my mother should open the door and smilingly announce that I had a visitor. "Colonel Morgan," she said. "He rode over from his place especially to see you."

Careless of the wound, I jumped up and followed her down the narrow stairway and across the hall to the parlor. There he was, standing talking with my father as he warmed his big back before the blaze in the fireplace. He was in Virginia Continentals, such a rig as I had never before seen him wear. My sister was listening with a fascinated expression. I strode across the room, fetched up before him, and saluted.

"My congratulations, sir, on the colonelcy. You sure earned it."

He grinned and grabbed my hand in a huge paw. "Must be the fine feathers," he rumbled. "A lot of times in the past you didn't bother about saluting me. How are you, Dave? You must have had a rough time,

from what I hear. That comes of joining up with Benedict Arnold's navy. I reckon you and him are trying to
fight the war too many ways."

His joking manner reminded me of the tales of a
young Morgan, riotous, betting on horse races, fist-
fighting for the fun of it. But he quickly reverted to the
Morgan I knew better, the serious, disciplined Morgan,
the driver of men and the knowing tactician.

"It was a great thing Arnold and you people did," he
said. "It's given us near on a year's time. We needed
it." He told us that he had been on the move through
northern Virginia recruiting for the new regiment, a
slow business. "I want the best. They've got to be smart
as well as good marksmen. I've taken only a hundred
eighty men so far. Governor Patrick Henry is impatient. He writes me that I'm too choosy. Maybe I am."

"I'd like to join up with you as soon as I can," I said.

"Good. Thought you would. The British are going
to invade from Canada again this year and God knows
what Howe will take it into his head to do. From New
York he can go up the Hudson to join forces with
Burgoyne, or he can use the fleet and his army to hit
the middle colonies. We're going to be busy. But it will
be summer before things really start moving. Take
your time. Get well. We'll need experienced men to
train the new ones. I'm getting in touch with most of
those left of the company. When you're ready there's a
sergeancy waiting for you in my regiment."

I thanked him, and my father asserted that if things
got bad he would enlist, too, as soon as the crops were
gathered.

Big Dan clapped him on the back, vowing that he was a tough old rooster and might be taken up on the offer. Mother looked worried. Morgan politely refused our invitation to dinner. He had to get to Winchester. Our stableman, Jim, bug-eyed with admiration, held his horse. As Morgan mounted he said, "Remember what I told you. Get plumb well. Then, if you're still of a mind to, come and join us. We'll be somewhere in Jersey."

Spring wrought its miraculous, almost overnight, transformation, covering the countryside with leaf and flower. It soon gave way to summer. One day around the middle of June I was strolling restlessly around the garden outside the house, feeling good in the warmth and admiring the clear outline of the mountains away to the east and west of the valley, when I saw someone approaching across the fields.

As I watched him, Caroline rushed out of the house. "It's Ben," she cried. "I declare, it is really Ben."

Hand in hand we walked to meet him.

"Why, you old busted-up soldier," he exploded, gripping my hand. "You're looking great, Dave. It's hard to believe when I remember what you were like in Albany back in the winter."

I assured him that I was feeling really perky again.

Ben's eyes widened and grew bright as he stared at Caroline. He took her hand and bowed over it, making his manners in a way that seemed strange when I remembered how my sister, two years younger than Ben and I, used to play the tomboy, trying to shinny up trees after us, sometimes beating us in a footrace, and always disputing our male superiority. Caroline was suddenly shy, and Ben as quickly turned awkward.

"You've changed," he told her. "Why, you've grown up almost—and—and you're real pretty, Caroline." There was no mistaking his admiration.

Two spots of red came into her cheeks. She made a curtsy, which startled me. "Thank you, sir," she said demurely. "We are very grateful for all you did for David."

He muttered something deprecatory. I looked at Caroline through new eyes. I was vaguely aware that now, on the verge of seventeen, she had grown into a beautiful girl since I had left home for the war. But, brotherlike, I had made no special mark of it, had rather taken it for granted. Evidently Ben had not. Well, well, I thought, how nice if . . .

With an effort, Ben recovered some of his usual aplomb.

"I'm down from Jersey on a short leave to pick up a squad of enlisters who are gathering at Winchester. We need more men."

"How is Big Dan making out with the regiment?"

"Fine. He's been whipping them into shape like nobody else could, but there wasn't enough of 'em, so he's got a new command now."

He explained that General Washington had just decided to form a special corps of at least 500 frontier rangers, every man a crack shot, and had appointed Morgan to command it. His Virginians were part of the regiment, the rest being men from Pennsylvania and

Maryland. They were intended to be elite troops for special assignments, with no usual camp duties to perform. Ben himself was now a sergeant.

"Golly, it sounds great," I exclaimed. "I think I'd better get ready to go back with you."

"But you aren't well enough yet," protested Caroline.

"No real hurry," said Ben. "You know Morgan. There'll be a lot of training. He'll teach these people what he taught us at Boston—in brushes with the British if he gets a chance."

At a family conference I was overruled three to one about going back with Ben. I agreed to wait another month. Even my mother conceded that I would be all right by then. So I fretted and fumed as the full heat of a stifling summer bore down upon the land. I went into Winchester, where I bought an excellent rifle and replenished my store of powder and ball.

Around the middle of July a report from the north reached the valley that the British were on the move again from Canada. Morgan's prediction was proved right. They were led by Gentleman Johnny Burgoyne who, so it was said, had managed to spend a comfortable winter in London, where he had presented a military plan to the King and no doubt had politicked his way into superseding Carleton as commander in chief of the army in Canada. The Redcoats were pushing up Lake Champlain, now undefended by any serviceable American vessels. The news had been more than two weeks on the way. It was time for me to move.

In a fine homemade rifleman's outfit, I took leave of

my dear family, my mother kissing me with grave tenderness, trying to hide her fears for me, my father wishing me luck and repeating that he might be along later, and Caroline tearfully hugging me and admonishing me to take good care of both myself and Ben. I set off alone toward the town and the long wagon road to Philadelphia.

15

BEMIS HEIGHTS

Colonel Daniel Morgan gave the order to halt. He looked around at the land. "It's a good place," he said to our captain. "Gates and the Polish fellow chose well."

Ben nodded. "He's right. It looks good."

We broke ranks and sat down to rest. We were on a plateau above the Hudson River. It was of varied height and was mostly forested, though there were a few small meadows and clearings here and there. Nearby was a deserted farmhouse. Another, with a log barn, stood farther away. Wooded, rising ground lay to the west. On the east the plateau sloped steeply down to the river. On the main road beside the Hudson was a tavern run by a man named Bemis, hence the name, Bemis Heights. To the north, beyond a meadow, I could make out two ravines. Past the second of these, I learned later, was a small abandoned farmhouse in a clearing known as Freeman's Farm. Both Bemis Heights and Freeman's Farm were names that would soon be famous.

197

"Don't see what's so good about it," said one of the men.

Our fellow sergeant, Jerry McGuire, looked critically at the speaker. "Mullins, your trouble is you don't use your eyes. 'Tis a fine place for rifles. Build a fort here above the river to stop Burgoyne if we can't stop him before that. But first, fight him out there. Trees to hide in and ridgy ground to help. Whether the Redcoats try to fight in the woods"—waving a hand at the woods and clearing north of us—"or in the open, people who shoot straight have an advantage. You got to learn to size up things better."

Ben grinned but said nothing. Jerry was developing into a rather stern disciplinarian.

The day was still and warm but already the forest was beginning to glow with reds and yellows. It seemed that always I was seeing the turning of leaves in this land—in Maine, on Champlain, and here on the Hudson. But things would be different now between us and our enemy. For what had been a dire threat to America when I set out from home in July had suddenly changed to at least an even struggle. Much had happened in the past two months.

I had joined Morgan's new regiment at Trenton. It had been hopping all over northern New Jersey helping to harass Sir William Howe's army of British and Hessians. Then Howe retired to New York and began putting troops aboard ships of the fleet commanded by his brother, Admiral Sir Richard Howe. What was his intention? Would he sail up the Hudson to join Burgoyne's thrust from Canada? That was said to be the British grand plan.

Morgan's men were ordered north to watch from the heights of the Hudson, but when the two Howes put to sea on July 23rd, the order was countermanded. Washington suspected the British aimed to attack Philadelphia from the Delaware or from Chesapeake Bay, and quickly gathered his army around the capital. That was why Morgan was at Trenton.

Affairs in the north, meanwhile, had gone from bad to worse. Burgoyne, with an army said to exceed 8,000, the bulk of it British and German (Brunswick) regulars, with Canadian, Indian, and Tory auxiliaries, and a huge train of guns, had taken Fort Ticonderoga. The outnumbered Americans under General Arthur St. Clair had retreated south with Burgoyne in hot pursuit. Past Skenesborough, where Arnold's boats had been built, the chase was slowed when General Schuyler set Americans to chopping down trees and laying them in tangled masses across the narrow, boggy road that stretched twenty-four miles to Fort Edward on the Hudson. But that had only delayed Burgoyne. His men had doggedly cleared the road foot by foot.

These things I learned from Ben and Jerry, who were among the few from the old company now in the regiment. They couldn't tell me anything about Caleb and Jean Claude except that they had stayed through the winter at Fort Ti. The rest at Trenton was welcome, but it hadn't lasted long.

More bad news from the north reached Washington, who dispatched Benedict Arnold to the scene. He also replaced General Schuyler as commander there with General Gates. Schuyler was a patriot and a gentleman who had spent much of his own money to feed and equip troops, but, aristocrat-like, he was said to be a bit highhanded at times. This was one of the reasons he had been unable to cope with Burgoyne; he was unpopular with the self-assertive New Englanders and his army was melting away. New Englanders, however, liked Gates and would serve under him.

On the heels of this change had come intelligence that a British force of 1,800, mostly Tories and Indians, had invaded the Mohawk Valley from Lake Ontario and laid siege to Fort Stanwix, aiming to press on to join Burgoyne at Albany. Local militia under a General Nicolas Herkimer, going to the aid of the fort, had been ambushed at Oriskany. They had rallied and fought well, but their commander had been mortally wounded. From Albany came desperate pleas for help.

So we were not greatly surprised when Washington ordered Morgan to go north and join Gates, who was en route to Albany. The Commander's letter contained high praise for the regiment. Washington wrote that he knew of no corps in proportion to its numbers so likely to check Burgoyne and deal with his Rangers and Indians, who terrified the militia. Making forced marches, we reached Peekskill on the Hudson, where schooners were to take us up the river. But unfavorable winds delayed us several days.

At Peekskill we heard of the victory at Bennington. Burgoyne had taken Fort Edward early in August and had reached a place barely forty miles above Albany. There he had halted, for he was having trouble getting enough supplies from Ticonderoga. Tories had told him of American military stores, cattle and horses, collected at Bennington in the Hampshire Grants. He had sent a column of Germans, accompanied by some Indian scouts, to seize them.

I could imagine the scene—German dragoons, dismounted for lack of horses, staggering through the August heat in their huge boots, bearing the heavy burden of their equipment and weapons, expecting little resistance, and suddenly finding themselves shot at from behind trees by militiamen under a resolute general named John Stark. Virtually all of them had been killed or captured. Later, a supporting column had been cut to pieces. The Germans had lost about 1,000 men.

We were jubilant. Militia were flocking to join the small army Gates had taken over from Schuyler. This was due in part to renewed confidence after Bennington, in part to the change of command, and in part to the tragic fate of Jane McCrea, whose pitiful story had been spread far and wide.

It had happened late in July. There were several versions of the story, but the gist of it was that Miss McCrea, who was engaged to a Tory officer with the British, had been staying with a friend near Fort Edward. Somehow or other she had fallen into the hands of some of Burgoyne's Indians and had been killed. One of the Indians had turned up at the British camp with her scalp, claiming she had been killed by a bullet fired by an American pursuer. Few believed him.

At any rate, the story hit home to the border people of New England and New York. It lent credence to the untrue charge that Burgoyne was a "hair buyer." Enraged farmers turned out in increasing numbers to fight him and his uncontrollable savages.

During our week-long stay at a camp near Albany Benedict Arnold, with 1,000 militia, had returned from the west after relieving Fort Stanwix and chasing the Tories and Indians back toward Canada. Continental troops were arriving and General Stark was gathering more men in the Grants. Arnold and Morgan set to work reorganizing the growing army. A corps of 300 picked musketmen under Major Henry Dearborn, the former captain on the march to Quebec, was added to Morgan's command.

Such was the chain of events which brought us, on this September afternoon, leading an army nearly 6,000 strong, to the place called Bemis Heights.

Our rest was brief. We pitched camp and unloaded baggage wagons as troops behind us arrived. Some of these were put to work digging trenches under the direction of a young military engineer from Poland named Thaddeus Kosciusko who had volunteered to fight for American freedom. The Gates-Kosciusko plan was to fortify part of the plateau with a three-sided series of interlocking and supporting bastions and redoubts for cannon and musketmen and link it to the river with other trenches. The main works and outlying redoubts would block the way between the river and the forest on our left. Kosciusko knew his business; in a few days the labor of a thousand men had built a formidable obstacle.

Morgan's men took little part in this effort. Our job

was to watch Burgoyne's army, which at this time was some miles to the north on the opposite side of the Hudson. We were to destroy bridges on the route of the army and, when opportunity came, tame its Rangers and Indians.

Five days after our arrival at Bemis Heights Burgoyne's army began to cross the river on a bridge of boats. It camped at Saratoga, on the river bank, where Gentleman Johnny set up headquarters in General Schuyler's mansion. Encumbered as he was with a lot of artillery and baggage, including a wagonload or two of his own champagne, he made slow progress. Operating in small groups, we had several tussles with his scouts, who got the worst of it because we could hide and pick them off at a distance. After a bit of this medicine they began to get fainthearted.

My company had just finished one of these little skirmishes and sent the scouts pelting back when I saw a curious movement of the underbrush about 50 yards away. At first I thought it might be due to a puff of wind, but after watching it closely I decided it was caused by somebody who was carefully crawling in our direction. I nudged Ben and drew a bead on the spot. Suddenly there was a rustle in the bushes nearby, and a voice spoke.

"No shoot!" it said urgently. "We friends. No shoot."

I whirled. Standing beside a sapling a few feet away was an Indian whose face was horrifically daubed with war paint. He threw down his musket and stared at me. "Dave!" he croaked.

I would not have recognized him under his paint,

but I knew the voice. "Mike!" I yelped. "What are you doing here?"

In a couple of jumps we bridged the distance between us to clasp hands. He turned. "It is good, brothers," he called.

From the spot I had been watching there popped up a figure in a rather indefinite costume consisting chiefly of faded blue coat and brown homespun pants. Close behind rose another clad in a patched, bedraggled British uniform.

"I'll be goldurned," said Caleb.

"*C'est incroyable,*" said Jean Claude.

There was quite a hubbuboo, with Ben hugging Jean Claude and Jerry jumping around pouring out a stream of excited words, and the rest of the company yapping demands to know what it was all about, and Caleb and Jean Claude and I all trying to talk at the same time while Mike stood beaming happily. It took a while to get things sorted out.

Yet their story was a simple one. Mike had turned up at Fort Ti during the spring, looking for me. When he learned that I was many leagues away recovering from wounds, he had attached himself to Caleb and Jean Claude. During Burgoyne's pursuit of St. Clair they had been cut off from the retreating Americans. Knowing nothing of what was happening beyond the advancing British, but determined to make contact with Americans, Caleb and Jean Claude had shed their uniforms and had posed as Tories who wanted to fight for the King. The three had played a dangerous game despite the care they took to avoid Hawknose and

Scarface and their superior, the harsh, cold-blooded La Corne St. Luc.

"We've got all the information you'll need about Burgoyne and his British and Germans, likewise his cannon," proclaimed Caleb. "We know what's happened to him since Bennington, and what he aims to do, hoping as he does that the British will come up from New York to help him."

"Morgan and Gates will be glad to hear it," I told him.

"There is something else," put in Jean Claude. "You with Morgan are—how you say—taking starch out of the Indians and Rangers. Some Indians even went back to Canada after Bennington. Others may follow. Keep it up. It is the only way to curb that devil St. Luc. Do you know what he said to the British, David? He said: 'It is necessary to let loose the savages against the miserable rebels, to impose terror on the frontier. *Il faut brutalizer les affaires.*' He meant men, women, and children, and he has been living up to his words."

"When we lick Burgoyne—" I began, then broke off. By that time our two enemies would probably be back in Canada. Anyway, now that we all had escaped their clutches, I had no particular desire ever to encounter them again, though I still hated them.

The morning of the 19th of September was clear and calm and quite chilly. We turned out at dawn, ready and watchful, for we knew that Burgoyne, plodding carefully forward, had camped for the night at a place between three and four miles north of us. Hampered by the timidity of his scouts, he probably wasn't sure of the position of the main American army, but he seemed determined to push on until he found it.

During the past several days we had sensed a certain indecision in our leadership. It was said that cautious General Gates—"that old woman," some called him— preferred to meet the British assault behind his entrenchments. Arnold, backed by Morgan, argued that the land favored an open battle to thin out the British rather than let them come at us full-force and pound us with artillery. Anyway, the trenches would be there if needed.

There were early reports from scouts of much activity in the British camp. Later in the morning watchers scrambled down from trees and came running in with news that Burgoyne was on the move. His army was advancing in three columns. One, containing a lot of Germans and artillery, was keeping to the river bank. Another was crossing a ravine toward our center. The third was taking a more inland route, aiming perhaps to turn our left flank in the woods. Tories and Indians accompanied the columns.

A council was held in the house General Gates occupied. It lasted quite a while. Finally Morgan strode out, looking like the cat that had caught the bird.

"Come on," he bawled. "We start the party. General Gates is depending on us. We're going to hit them."

We set up a yell and followed him across the meadow in front of the fortifications. Morgan formed us in two thin lines and stationed himself just back of the second. It was like the old days of training at Cambridge. Behind us Dearborn's regiment moved out in support. The time was well past noon.

Lieutenant Colonel Richard Butler commanded the advance, which was led by a detachment under Major Jacob Morris of Maryland. We set out in double file on a wagon track bordered by underbrush. As we left I could see other troops forming in the meadow—General Enoch Poor's New Hampshire men and regiments from New York, Massachusetts, and Connecticut. A lot of others stayed on to hold the fort.

The advance force set off at a rapid pace and soon lost contact with the rest of us. A single cannon shot boomed to the north. Morgan hurried us on, thinking this a British signal for the attack.

We had gone about a mile when we heard a ripple of firing ahead. This was followed by faintly heard triumphant yells. After a bit there was another spatter of rifle shots and then the dull crashes of British volleys fired at short intervals. Morgan broke into a run. We pelted after him.

Soon a rifleman dashed out of the woods and tried to cross our line. "We're ruined," he gasped. Ben tripped him sprawling to the ground and demanded to know what had happened.

Before the confused fellow could reply we heard the *gobble-gobble* of Morgan's turkey call. It went on and on, signaling the riflemen to rally to its sound. When we caught up with him he was near to tears in his rage and humiliation. He was tootling on his turkey bone, then swearing savagely, then tootling again. General Gates's self-important adjutant, Wilkinson, now a colonel, came dashing up on a horse. "It's bad," Morgan exclaimed to him. "My men are scattered everywhere."

But it was better than it seemed. Soon flustered riflemen of the advance gathered around Morgan. They had suffered very little save in morale. We learned they had surprised a detachment of Burgoyne's advance guard. That was the first firing we had heard. 'It had wrecked the British detachment. Happily pursuing the enemy, the riflemen had come into the clearing known as Freeman's Farm—and had run smack into the center column of Redcoats, under Burgoyne himself.

"Caught a Scotch prize," Colonel Butler told Morgan, meaning he'd had the worst of it.

"When they began them volleys we took off like partridges," admitted a rifleman glumly. "Didn't know I could run so fast."

"It's all right, now," growled Morgan, vastly relieved. "Form lines again. We're going to meet them. Use your heads! Take cover and make every shot count. We'll see how much good their volleys will do 'em."

Soon we reached the edge of the clearing, halted, and kept in the brush. Some men climbed trees. Morgan stationed the companies to right and left, communicating with the captains by turkey call. Dearborn's corps joined us, extending our line.

In front of us, in a clearing about 350 yards long, was an English artillery battery and behind it three regiments, lined up as if on parade. In the pine woods beyond the clearing another regiment stood in reserve. Mindful of Morgan's orders to concentrate on officers and artillerymen, we took careful aim, for the range was pretty long even for rifles. Here and there Redcoats began to fall.

The British knew they could not reach us with musket fire, but they were not the sort of people to take this without retaliating. The battery opened on us with grapeshot. The blasts raked the ·trees, sending limbs crashing down. But the gunners were shooting blind, for our hunting shirts made us all but invisible in the woods, and we suffered little damage. We kept pecking away.

General Poor's New Hampshire Continentals were coming in to line, extending our left flank toward the place where we expected the British right column. Other regiments were coming up. Arnold was throwing in as many troops as he could beg from Gates.

We were doing a lot of hurt to the artillerymen and the three regiments in the clearing. Suddenly the British pulled back to the shelter of the woods behind them. Poor's Continentals and Dearborn's corps rushed out to seize the guns. But the cannoneers had taken their linstocks with them, so the guns were useless. The British crashed two quick volleys at the Americans, then came out in a bayonet charge. Poor's and Dearborn's men had time for one volley before they broke and retreated to the woods.

The fight went on like that for about two hours. Every time the remaining cannoneers came back we would get a few more of them. Every time the regiments came out to regain the guns from our musketmen we would get more of their officers and men. The fel-

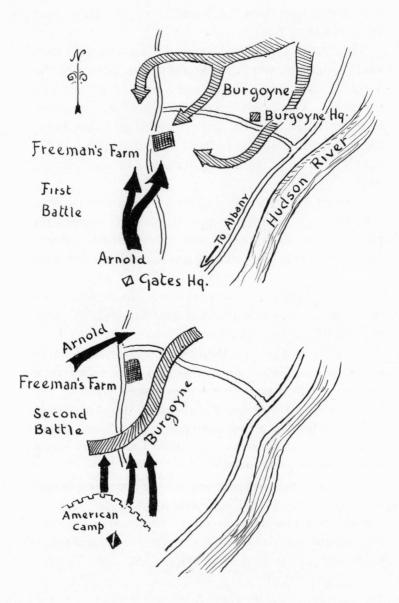

lows were calling their shots. "I've got the officer on the bay horse," one would say. "No, you haven't, I've got him," another would answer. Two rifles cracked as one. The officer toppled off the horse. Then there was bitter argument as to which shot had hit him.

At midafternoon the cannon shots, the musketry and the rifle fire reached a climactic din. Troops on our extended left flank were probing between the British center and right column. I could see them working around the flank of the regiments facing us. To meet the threat, the regiment nearest them changed front. This forced the center regiment, which we later learned was the 62nd, to shift to the right, exposing both flanks.

Morgan quickly took advantage of the opportunity.

Yelling for us to concentrate our fire on that regiment, he led us into the open to get nearer. Dearborn's men came with us. We shot as fast as we could reload and aim. What was left of the 62nd melted in swaths of dead and wounded. The survivors, with only a few officers left to steady them, were on the verge of breaking in panic when the other two regiments came to the rescue. They poured volleys at us and made a bayonet charge. We retired to the woods.

A bullet on the last volley had nicked Ben on the arm. It was a mere scratch, but I put a bandage on to stop the blood. Ben didn't seem to mind it, though he was mad about the rent in his sleeve. A couple of others in the company were wounded, but not seriously.

"I reckon they can say when they get back home that they got a good dustin' today," crowed one of the company.

"They ain't never goin' to get home," said Jerry grimly. "Can't you see that from what's happenin'?"

British officers who lived through that afternoon vowed later that in all their experience on European battlefields during the Seven Years War they had never met such withering fire.

For a time there was a lull. Burgoyne's center column was in desperate plight, his guns silenced, most of the gunners dead or wounded. The 62nd had been cut to pieces; three-fourths of its men were gone. The other regiments had taken heavy losses. Yet the fighting was resumed in a desultory way, with fruitless attacks and counterattacks.

Late in the afternoon, as the Americans set themselves to move in and finish the job, help came for the British. General von Riedesel, with a battery of artillery and several regiments from the column that had come down along the river, arrived. His appearance stiffened the British, and the combined forces drove the Americans back out of the bloody clearing. But we stayed in the woods nearby.

At dusk firing flared briefly on the left. Then there was silence on the battlefield—silence broken by the moans of wounded men.

Ben and Jerry and I found Caleb's and Jean Claude's company a short distance away. The two were excited over what they called our victory.

"Gentleman Johnny doesn't seem to know it yet, but he's licked," said Caleb jubilantly. "One more to go and we'll have him."

"It is the way to fight, with the rifle in the woods— *magnifique!*" cried Jean Claude.

"He's cornered," agreed Jerry. "He's gettin' weaker an' we're gettin' stronger every day."

"We could have had him this time if Gates had given us the men," commented Caleb. "Looks like Arnold threw his whole division in, but Gates was holding back. We did this with less than half our army. And the British lost at least twice as many men as we did."

"You can thank the Old Wagoner for most of that, for the training he gave us and the way he handled things," added Ben. "Poor and Dearborn helped a lot. I don't know how we'd have done without them, but it was mainly the rifle."

The night was freezing. We expected another attack

in the morning, but when daylight came it seeped through a thick fog that obscured everything. Sounds of chopping came from the British lines. Burgoyne was building fortifications. When the fog cleared we went back to our entrenchments.

So ended the battle known both as Freeman's Farm and the First Saratoga. The latter seems to me a misnomer, since the village of Saratoga lies on the river eight or nine miles north of where we fought.

16

VICTORY

For the next seventeen days the two armies lay a mile apart watching each other. The British built half a dozen redoubts, extending from ground overlooking the Hudson west to Freeman's farm. One redoubt was near the Freeman house, another was a quarter of a mile to the northwest, at the end of the British line.

This was a busy time for riflemen. We enfiladed the enemy camps from treetops, potshot at their sentries, raided their outposts at night. Our object was to wear down their nerves, giving them no rest from alarms day or night.

Soon after the first battle a messenger had galloped into camp with good news. Dependable General Benjamin Lincoln of New Hampshire, who earlier had been sent to gather militia in New England, had collected a force of 1,500 and set out to attack Ticonderoga. His men surprised and took two of the heights near the fort, burned some British vessels and 200 transport bateaux, liberated 100 Americans and captured 300 prisoners. They hadn't taken the fort but had inflicted great damage in loss of supplies. Burgoyne would now be short of rations. We celebrated with yells and a considerable waste of powder.

In spite of this blow Gentleman Johnny still could have retreated and perhaps have saved his army, but, according to a deserter, he clung stubbornly to the delusion that Clinton was leading a British army from New York to join him. That *had* been the British plan, but something must have gone amiss, else Howe, Clinton's superior, would not have sailed from New York. Much too late Clinton advanced timidly up the Hudson, took Fort Montgomery and burned Kingston, then lingered aimlessly and helped Burgoyne not a bit. It was no way to fight a war.

We Americans were having troubles of our own. Arnold's greatest fault was his ability to make enemies; he was forever complaining of intriguers who were out to tarnish his fame. In the Gates-Schuyler conflict which had led to Gates being given the northern command, Arnold had tended to side with the aristocrat Schuyler. This resulted in growing animosity between Arnold and Gates, which had now become an open quarrel. It was perhaps only natural, considering Arnold's impetuosity and Gates's combination of ambition and caution. Gates had relied chiefly upon Morgan in the recent battle; he had kept Arnold from taking much active part in it.

Now the two were at daggers' points. Gates ordered Morgan to make reports directly to him, bypassing Arnold. Arnold learned that Gates had not mentioned

his division—the only one that fought—in his report to
Congress. There were hot words. Arnold threatened
to rejoin Washington. Gates invited him to do so. Instead, Arnold sulked and stirred up trouble among
some New York officers who were friends of Schuyler.
Gates took over Arnold's division, stripping him of
authority. This, also, was no way to fight a war.

Yet daily we grew stronger as more militia arrived.
When Burgoyne made his next move, we were double
our original 6,000. Meanwhile another plume was added to the feathers of self-esteem sprouting on Morgan's
corps. Washington, hard pressed by Howe's army of
15,000 which had landed at the head of Chesapeake
Bay and advanced on Philadelphia, asked that we be
released from northern service to help him. Gates sent
a courier racing back with a message declaring the
outcome still uncertain and pleading that "Your Ex-
cellency would not wish me to part with the corps the
army of General Burgoyne are most afraid of."

On the morning of October 7th Gentleman Johnny's
chilled and by now hungry army began its final futile
effort to break through to Albany. Scouts discovered
that 1,500 men were marching into a wheatfield three-
quarters of a mile south and a little west of Freeman's
Farm. Time passed while the move was investigated.
Gates's adjutant, Wilkinson, gave the opinion that the
British might be probing our left flank, offering battle.
Wilkinson conferred with Gates, then talked with Morgan.

The Old Wagoner had his own idea of what the

move meant. He knew the terrain thoroughly. "Seems like Burgoyne thinks there's a height some place over there where he could mount guns," he told Wilkinson. "What comes of us blinding his scouts so much. There's a hill all right, but it's wooded and no good for artillery. That gives me a notion. We can grab it and flank him." He was silent for a moment, thinking.

"Tell the General I propose to crawl my corps and Dearborn's through the brush until we're where we can hit them on their right flank. If he'll send somebody—General Poor's Continentals maybe, they're good—to hit the other flank, we'll clamp a pincer on them. Give us time to get there and get set—it's about a mile and a half. When Poor begins the game I'll strike."

Gates approved the plan, terming it admirable, though I think he might have done so with any plan Morgan proposed, so much did he rely on Big Dan's brains and fighting ability.

The riflemen filed out of the clearing near the fortifications and entered the woods in the usual two-line march formation. Our company was the last to leave, with Morgan tramping alongside. At length, circling quietly through the undergrowth we reached an elevation overlooking the western end of the wheatfield. The woods here were filled with those who had preceded us, all silent, waiting. A ravine made by a brook lay along the southern edge of the field, which was about a thousand yards long, east to west. White-stemmed birch trees grew in the ravine. A worm fence separated the cleared ground from the woods. Another fence extended along the north side of the field. The field itself was studded with stumps, showing it was newly cleared.

The British were sitting in the field in double ranks waiting for orders. Those nearest us wore the scarlet coats and the little black leather hats of the light infantry. They were a crack corps led, as we knew, by the Earl of Balcarres. Beyond them, in the center, were Germans in blue coats. The far flank was held by British grenadiers who were recognizable, even in the distance, by their tall bearskin hats. They were commanded by a Major Acland, one of Burgoyne's cardplaying, wine-drinking companions. Ten cannon stood in the field. From the roof of a little cabin British and German officers were scanning the woods through spyglasses.

Morgan quietly passed orders back to Dearborn. As soon as Poor attacked, the rifle corps would strike Balcarres's flank and rear. While the light infantry were trying to dispose themselves to meet the blow, Dearborn would hit what was now their front. We waited tensely.

Some time later—it must have been near midafternoon—a mass of Americans, their figures tiny in the distance, boiled up from a ravine on the far flank and made for the grenadiers. Musketry rattled and cannon boomed. Smoke suddenly obscured the scene.

Morgan's turkey call gobbled. "Here we go, boys!" he howled.

We answered with shrill yells as we swept to the edge of the field, vaulted the fence, and began peppering the British. Balcarres's men, brave and capable, tried to change front, which is easy on a drill field but difficult under a surprise attack. Many of their officers fell in the first moments. Quickly the troops became a shuffling, disorganized mass. At this point Dearborn's men dashed from the wooded ravine and ripped an accurate volley into the huddled British. They followed with a bayonet charge as we shot those who tried to stand. The field was covered with dead and wounded. The survivors broke and fled. In the woods beyond the second fence Balcarres managed to rally them.

Leaving Dearborn to deal with them, Morgan led us streaming toward the Germans in the center of the field. "Come on!" he bellowed furiously. "We've got them." We ran in no sort of order, stopping to shoot as we pleased and reloading as we darted from stump to stump.

The Germans, under their chubby but thoroughly efficient Baron von Riedesel, were stanch troops. They had cannon and were now on guard. They gave us a hot fire. Under it, Morgan suddenly changed tactics, began waving back the more eager riflemen. "Hold it awhile," he yelled. "Take to the ground. Keep cracking at 'em." He was staring intently at the ravine south of the Germans.

In a moment we heard cheering from that direction. Americans with the crossed belts of Continentals on their chests bounded up the slope out of the white-stemmed birches in the hollow, halted for one volley at the Germans, then charged.

Caleb, who in the mix-up of companies was nearby, shouted, "It's General Ebenezer Learned's brigade. Now we'll see."

His assurance was premature. German cannons roared and musketry rattled. Through the sudden clouds of white smoke I saw the Americans hesitate, then turn and run back to the ravine.

Our advance had halted. Crouching low behind stumps and dead trees, we picked at the Germans. They turned a cannon on us but the grapeshot whistled harmlessly over our heads. We were so close we could hardly miss. The Brunswickers wavered. Their remaining officers went up and down ranks hitting men with the flats of their swords to keep them steady.

Suddenly the ravine erupted Americans again. At their head was a man on a brown mare. He wore a blue and buff uniform. He waved his sword forward and screeched encouragement. I recognized the stocky figure and swarthy face of Benedict Arnold. The crouching riflemen stared, then gave a great yell. The Continentals, bayonets fixed, drove at the Germans. The outnumbered Brunswickers retreated rapidly across the field and into the woods. Arnold led Learned's men after them.

During the lull that followed we wondered about Arnold. It was Jerry's opinion that Gates had not sent him, that, instead, he had defied Gates. Ben agreed. "He's been mighty restless and he's not the kind to keep out of action."

We could now see what had happened on the British left flank. The grenadiers had vanished. Some of General Poor's men were carrying away wounded. One of them came running to us.

"We licked the lobsterbacks," he shouted gleefully. "We stopped their charge with one volley and grabbed one of their guns and turned it on 'em. They broke and ran. We got their leader, Major Acland. Shot through both legs. Our boys have just carried him away."

Again we yelled in triumph. Dan Morgan's pincer tactic had beaten Burgoyne to a frazzle.

Morgan's turkey call brought us back to our business. It wasn't over yet. British infantry still held the worm fence north of the field. The British were shooting between the rails; bullets zipped around us. An officer on a gray horse rode among scattered British troops beyond the fence, rallying them, forming them into lines.

"That is General Simon Fraser," Jean Claude called to me. "He is one of their best. Very brave."

Morgan pointed to the man on the gray horse. "If we don't get him, he'll get us," he shouted.

Riflemen ran to a clump of trees in the field and began climbing them. Others knelt, sighting. The target was a long shot away—too long, perhaps. Rifles cracked.

The British General turned his head, looking down at his horse's crupper as if he thought something had hit it. An aide gestured urgently and tried to spur in front of him. A rifle spat from one of the trees, then spat again. The General clutched his stomach and slowly bent over the horse's neck. The aide seemed to be holding him there as two soldiers led the horse away.

The shot that mortally wounded Fraser was credited to Tim Murphy, an Indian fighter and fine marksman.

He had an unusual weapon—a double-barreled rifle—which was why he could fire again so quickly after his first shot.

We rushed toward the fence. Disheartened by the loss of their leader, the British scrambled pell-mell through the woods and back to their main fortifications. All this had happened, strange to say, in less than an hour after the first attack had been launched.

Morgan now took the lead. We pressed on to the edge of Freeman's Farm. There we came upon many Americans who were trying to sort themselves out and find their commands after their disordered pursuit of the enemy. Arnold on his brown mare was haranguing them.

To our right, near the Freeman house, stood a formidable earthwork protected by an abatis of sharpened tree trunks. The snouts of cannon pointed out from embrasures. This was the Balcarres redoubt, one of those Burgoyne had built since the first battle. The last of the retreating British were pouring into it. On a slight elevation to the northwest, at the end of the British line, was the other equally strong redoubt named for the German General von Breymann. It was manned by blue-coated Brunswickers. In a swale between these positions were two cabins.

Arnold saw Morgan and cantered his horse to him. "I'm going for that redoubt," he said, pointing at the Balcarres fort. "Why don't you go for the other? If we can take both of them, that does it."

Morgan nodded. "It was on my mind," he said grimly. "But you be careful. They're in the bag now.

You're touchy, and you're quite a target. No use getting yourself killed."

"That would make little difference to me now," replied Arnold in his high-pitched voice.

Working around to the west and south of the Breymann redoubt, we came under a heavy fire of grape and canister and hugged the ground. Slowly we crept toward the works, shooting at any defender who showed his head.

Arnold had gathered troops and was leading them on his prancing mare against the Balcarres redoubt. They followed him in a howling mass, as more and more militia poured from the woods behind them. The Americans got to the abatis and tried to claw through it but it was too much for them. A great din of cannon and small arms filled the air. Men were being killed to no purpose. Arnold led troops against the upper side of the redoubt, rode back in a hail of bullets, and marshaled men out of the abatis to join the others.

Morgan was studying the approaches to the German fort. Just beneath it was a small ravine. The slope up to the earthwork, its abatis, and the stockade on top of the earthwork was short but steep. Some of our men got into the ravine, which offered shelter from the fire above but was impractical as a route by which to storm the fort. The best way to take the place seemed to be from the south, where the ground was almost level.

The day was growing clouded and gray. The short October afternoon was passing. Filled with a sense of urgency, two companies of us were following Morgan to the level ground from which we planned to attack, when we saw Arnold dash away from the fruitless fighting at the Balcarres redoubt straight across the line of fire, like a man possessed.

We stopped gape-mouthed to watch. By all odds he and his mare should have been hit a dozen times, but his luck held. He reached Learned's brigade and swept it swirling toward the cabins between the redoubts. Musket fire flashed from the cabins. The Americans ran on. Green-clad Canadians tumbled out of the cabins and ran helter-skelter into the forest.

Morgan roared for us to follow him. We raced to the east side of the redoubt, saw an open sally port, and swarmed in. Arnold and his Continentals reached the entrance just behind us.

"Clean them out," shrieked Arnold. "We've got a half hour before dark."

All was confusion in the redoubt. We crouched behind wagons near the sally port and started shooting. The Germans rushed us. We smashed at their bayonets and their heads with our rifle butts. The Continentals met bayonet with bayonet, slashing and stabbing. Morgan bawled something but we couldn't understand him in the din.

Panic gripped the Brunswickers. Some threw down their arms and sought escape over the stockade. I saw a German officer cut down three of his men as he tried to stop their flight. Another soldier fired point-blank at the officer's chest. The man he shot, we soon learned, was General von Breymann.

The place was a shambles. A group of Germans, trapped against the north parapet, continued to fight.

Some of their bullets hit Arnold and his mare. The mare went down, pawing the air. When we got to Arnold to free him of her weight we saw blood spreading from a leg wound. It was the left leg, the same that had taken the musket ball at Quebec.

"I wish it had struck my heart," he groaned.

Much has been said during the remaining years of the War for Independence about Benedict Arnold's role in the Battle of Second Saratoga. Those whose views are colored by Arnold's later treachery to the American cause, which has made his name a symbol of infamy, would deny him his just due. Others, romantics, bedazzled by the tale of his dramatic gesture, would grant him all the credit for winning this battle. The truth, as so often, lies between.

Having witnessed it all, I can only say that on that afternoon Arnold, driven by egotism, ambition, and hatred of Gates and his other enemies, did a desperate thing which seemed to him heroic but to me foolish. His assault on the redoubts made little difference in the outcome; that had been decided earlier in the wheatfield. It might have taken another day, but we would have beaten Burgoyne anyway. The Arnold of the second battle was not the Arnold of Valcour Island. He was taken to the hospital in Albany where he recovered and later rejoined the army around Philadelphia.

On the next day Burgoyne lingered behind his eastern entrenchments. The British buried General Fraser. We pressed them with cannon fire and raids on their outposts. They had lost 600 men; our loss was 150.

That night, leaving campfires burning to deceive us, Gentleman Johnny, dragging his cannon with him, began his slow, hopeless retreat up the Hudson. Gates acted promptly. With plenty of troops to spare, he sent regiments around Burgoyne on both sides of the river, blocking the way to the north. The end was near.

When the Americans took possession of the main British camp in a heavy rain on the following morning they found 500 enemy wounded Burgoyne had left behind under a British surgeon. Gates ordered that they be given good care. Our pursuit was slow, for the cold rain continued; the road, churned to muck by the retreat, was cluttered with broken carts; and the British had burned the bridges. Burgoyne reached Saratoga and spent the night in Schuyler's mansion. Early the next morning he moved his army across Fishkill Creek and set fire to Schuyler's house, barn, and mill.

We brought up cannon and on October 10th pounded at the British, who had thrown up entrenchments around a few houses standing on high ground north of the Fishkill. Gates was in no hurry.

It was well that he wasn't, because on the next day we narrowly escaped serious trouble. Hearing a report that Burgoyne and much of his army had decamped toward Fort Edward, Gates planned to have Morgan attack what was thought to be the rearguard and then lead the chase. That morning thick fog obscured the scene. We groped through it to the bank of the creek where we waited for better conditions before beginning the fight.

Just as the fog began to lift orders came from Gates

to abandon the attack. A British deserter had con-
vinced him that Burgoyne's army was still there,
strongly placed, with plenty of cannon. The rumor that
Gentleman Johnny had retreated apparently was based
on the fact that he had sent some troops and a party of
Tory workmen to bridge the Hudson near Fort Edward.
Subsequently we learned that these had run into militia
and had a lively scrap which had sent the workmen
fleeing back to Burgoyne.

So American artillery got to work again from the
south and from across the Hudson. Our gunners put a
lot of shell holes in the three or four houses in the
midst of the enemy camp, kept the British crouched in
their trenches, and in general made their life miserable.
Meanwhile, Morgan shifted the eight companies of his
corps to the rear of Burgoyne's fortification, to cut off
Rangers and Indians and any others who tried to get
away.

17

THE CABIN IN THE WOODS

It was time for Morgan's move. In the forest northwest of Burgoyne's position we flushed a number of Tories and a few Rangers and Indians who were quitting the defeated army. We captured two British infantrymen, who declared that Burgoyne had passed the word that any soldiers who, singly or in small groups, wanted to try to escape to Ticonderoga were free to do so.

This put a new face on the situation. If true, it indicated more disintegration of the enemy than we had expected. It also vastly complicated our task of covering the considerable area through which the deserters might make their way. Morgan ordered four of his companies to keep watch on Burgoyne. The other four would break up into groups of eight or ten men and scour the woods. We would not have much rest, he said, for we'd need to be alert day and night, but it was necessary.

On the afternoon of the next day Ben, Jerry, and I, with seven others of our company were patrolling the

woods when we heard a faint sound that indicated
somebody was approaching. We took cover. In a moment I saw Jean Claude appear from behind a spruce.
Caleb and Mike followed him. I stifled an impulse to
shout "Boo" at them.

"Well, see who it is," exclaimed Caleb as we made
known our presence.

"What are you doing here?" I demanded, for their
company was one of the four left to watch Burgoyne.

"Looking for Morgan," he replied. "D'ye know his
whereabouts?"

"No. He's supposed to be with you folks."

"He got restless last night. Come dawn, he went out
with three men to do some scouting, I calculate. Now
Gates wants him. Sent a message for him to come to
headquarters. That's why we're looking for him."

"A fine howdydo," commented Jerry. "Says he trusts
us to take care of ourselves, then he goes traipsin'
around the woods without sense enough to take care
of his own self."

Annoyed but not worried, we split into smaller
parties in order to cover more ground. Five men struck
off toward the west. Jerry, Caleb, Jean Claude, and
Mike elected to go north. Ben and I, with Pete Burns
and John Ray, took a northwesterly direction between
the routes of the other groups.

We had searched for an hour, the four of us spread
out but keeping in touch, when I heard a moan. Signaling to the others, I followed the sound and came upon
the body of an Indian, a Huron by his looks. Beside
him lay a dead rifleman who had been scalped. Ten feet
away sat one of our men who had managed to drag

himself to a tree and prop his back against it. He had been shot in a lung. He seemed in a bad way.

"Thank God you've come," he gasped through a froth of blood. "They got us . . . got Dan Morgan."

"Gct Morgan!" I cried, not believing him.

"Ambushed . . . Rangers and Injuns . . . fifteen or twenty."

Between labored breaths he told his story. He and two companions had left camp with Morgan at first daylight. They had circled for hours, had had a brush with a few Indians who had escaped. Later, they had been surprised by the hidden gang. The rifleman had accounted for several before the other two were slain and he was wounded. The rest had set on Morgan. He had disposed of two with his knife, had broken another's head against a tree, had flung them off like terriers. Through my horror I could see Big Dan in action.

"Then one of 'em . . . leader, I think . . . got behind him . . . broke a musket butt over his head. . . . Morgan went down like a sledgehammered ox . . . husky feller, the other . . . scar on one cheek."

Ben's eyes met mine. The sutler again? The man was definite about the scar. The rest of his description left no doubt.

Grimly we examined the place of combat. In the brush we found the bodies of another rifleman, three Rangers, and three Indians. Which way had the captors taken Morgan? The wounded man gestured in the general direction we had been going. We picked up the trail. It was easy to follow. Carrying the weight of Big Dan they couldn't help making a clear trail.

I told Pete and John to make a litter of rifles and tree

branches and take the wounded man to camp. I feared he wouldn't live to get there, but it was the only thing we could do for him. They must come back quickly with help. I showed them the trail we were taking. Without another word Ben and I began to follow it.

There was no trouble except in a couple of places where we had to cast around until we picked up footprints in soft ground. We snapped twigs and small branches of trees, leaving them dangling as signs for those we hoped would follow. As we went on I wondered about the reason for the ambush. If they had meant to kill Morgan why hadn't they done it then and there? No, those two devils—for I was sure Hawknose was in this too—had some other purpose. The track led on and on. It was growing late; the light from the overcast sky was fading. Soon it would be dark.

Suddenly Ben, who was leading, froze, then slumped softly to the ground. I did the same. Peering ahead, I could barely see in the deepening shadows a log cabin in a tiny clearing. The trail led through bracken, which was broken where they had trod, to its door. This was the end of the search.

We lay, waiting for full dark. It was a time for patience, the long-enduring patience of the hunter. As night crept in we shivered in the damp mid-October cold.

A candle was lighted in the cabin. Its faint glow could be seen through a small window or opening facing us. With infinite caution we began to creep toward the cabin, making sure that no rustles came from the carpet of new-fallen leaves beneath us.

When we got there we found the window was merely an opening with a hinged shutter, now propped half open. We lay in the bracken listening. I heard a murmur of voices speaking French. At times they were high enough and clear enough for me to make out what was being said. One voice asked when the Major would be sent for. Scarface's mumbled reply was: "When this one regains his senses and can talk."

"You should not have struck so hard," grumbled the other. "What if they come upon us and find him?"

"Be silent," said Scarface sharply.

I raised myself until I could peer through the opening. The one room of the cabin seemed filled with men. Scarface crouched on a stool watching Morgan, who lay in a corner. He seemed to be bound. Sitting or squatting on the floor were four Rangers and five Indians. Hope of rushing them faded; odds of ten to two were impossible. I whispered my findings to Ben.

The night wasn't completely black, for the moon was up, though little of its light penetrated the overcast. There was no way to tell time. Each moment seemed an hour. What could we do?

A considerable while later I was jerked from my thoughts by the shrill voice of a Ranger who exclaimed, "Aha, he revives." Peering over the windowsill, I saw Morgan struggle to sit upright. He shook his head in puzzlement and looked dully at his captors. Then he gave a great roar and burst into eloquent curses. He was in a thorough rage.

Scarface yelled something to him but I couldn't hear what he said through all the noise Big Dan was making.

Four of the men threw themselves on Morgan, trying to gag him. One of them jumped back with a howl of pain, waving a bitten finger. The others managed to bind a cloth over the prisoner's mouth but he could still make inarticulate noises through it. I was much relieved to see him so alive and kicking.

The man with the scar said something to one of the Rangers, who beckoned to an Indian. The two left the cabin and headed north. I assumed they were going to summon Hawknose.

Ben and I conferred in whispers. There were now eight enemies in the cabin. We could get two of them with bullets and, with luck, two more with knives. But there would still be four. And Morgan couldn't help until we unbound him. It was too risky.

We continued our silent vigil. Morgan subsided, though his eyes glared defiance. Bored, the remaining Rangers began playing cards. The Indians squatted impassively. Scarface sat on the stool watching the prisoner.

It was around midnight, I suppose, when we heard someone swishing through the bracken to the door of the cabin. Hawknose, resplendent in a blue uniform, entered. He and Scarface exchanged words. "We have the prize, you see," said the latter.

"Very good. Now to business."

"What happened to the two I sent to tell you?"

"They were hungry and needed rest. They will be along later."

Scarface spoke to Morgan. "Listen, Colonel, we have a matter to discuss with you. There's no use yelling your head off. We don't want to hurt you. Why, you're as safe here as you would be in your own camp. Be reasonable and listen. We'll get along better that way."

His manner was false-friendly, just as it had been in the meadow at Cambridge. At his signal a Ranger unbound the cloth over Morgan's mouth.

"What d'ye have to say to me?" growled Big Dan. He was having a hard time controlling his anger.

The man who called himself Tremaine answered. "I need scarcely tell you, Colonel, that General Burgoyne and his army are, let us say, in some danger from General Gates and his rabble. You are now in our hands. I do not mean to flatter you, but in truth you are the most valuable prisoner we could have taken— worth a dozen generals. And Gates knows it." He paused. "What I propose is simply this," he continued. "You will write a note to Gates saying that you are held captive by desperate men, at a place he could never find, as hostage for Burgoyne's army. If he will let Burgoyne retreat to Ticonderoga and there take boats to Canada you will be freed the moment Burgoyne reaches Fort Edward."

Morgan's expression showed his astonishment. "Go to the devil," he snapped.

Tremaine tried again. "It is a fair deal," he said persuasively. "And it would certainly be to your interest, for while we mean you no harm, our actions are contingent upon yours." He paused. When he spoke next his voice was silky smooth. "I regret to say that if you refuse to write this note you will never be heard of again. You are not popular with our Indians, you know . . ."

"If you think Gates would be fool enough to agree to such a proposal you are dead wrong. Never."

"Perhaps he wouldn't, but there is a chance he would. At any rate, we can but try. A desperate plight calls for a desperate remedy. I have pen and paper ready."

"No, blast you," said Morgan.

It went on like that for quite a time. My hair was fair standing straight in fright. Tremaine sounded determined.

Morgan was speaking again. "Maybe you think I don't know about you and your helper there. I'm ashamed of doubting Gordon's story even for a moment. You did us damage about Quebec. But now you're through."

"Not yet," smiled the man. "Not yet."

"You call yourself Tremaine, but that's not your name."

I couldn't tell whether Morgan was actually curious or was just talking for time, hoping something would happen.

"Your interest in me is amusing," replied the other coldly. "Well, we have the night for it. Meanwhile, reflect on your situation."

Morgan continued. "The real Tremaine has never been seen since the time you turned up at Washington's headquarters playing his part."

"That was rather a near thing, wasn't it?" said Hawk-nose with satisfaction. "I didn't care to see Arnold that morning; I had disposed of Tremaine the previous day. Not that I had much against the fellow except I suspected he and Arnold together had done me out of a plantation in Jamaica some years before. I killed him because it was necessary to my plans."

"Why the plans? Why have you risked your neck for the British?"

The man smiled again. "Very compelling reasons, my dear Colonel. They can be summed up in two words —wealth and power. When you rebels are at last put down I will have a vast domain in western Pennsylvania. That has been promised by Lord Germain himself. My assistant and I will rule an area that will make the holdings of Johnson of the Mohawks here in New York seem meager indeed."

"You see, we haven't got any use for what you call patriotism," rumbled Scarface. "It doesn't get you anything. Land and money, that's what counts and that we'll have."

"Why, you dirty scoundrels!" exploded Morgan. He was off again in a swearing tirade that put to shame his earlier effort. I was afraid he would burst a blood vessel. But it didn't last. Rangers tied the cloth over his mouth, knotting it viciously at the back of his neck.

"Now you can cool off and think a little while," Hawknose told him. "But," he added ominously, "only a little while." He spoke to a Ranger. "Take an Indian with you. Get to General Burgoyne. Go by the river way. It is easier to slip by Yankee sentries there. Tell the General I have Morgan as hostage for the safe retreat of the army. Tell him I think I can persuade the

Colonel to send the right message to Gates. He can leave that to me. He should be in readiness. I will communicate with him later."

The Ranger and an Indian departed. Hawknose's meaning was clear. If necessary he would torture his prisoner. Ben and I whispered together. Seven men remained in the cabin. Should we take a chance? Ben counseled caution, for a while at least.

An hour or more passed. It was still quite a while until daylight. Suddenly the unforeseen but hoped-for happened.

The sound of several shots, with intervals between them, broke the night's stillness. They were from the direction of the river and some distance away. A moment later there followed a rapid spatter of firing.

The effect on those in the cabin was instantaneous. "Guard the prisoner," Hawknose ordered one of the two Rangers. "The rest spread out. Take posts a hundred paces from here. Shoot anything that moves. Close the door behind you." He led the way.

It all happened so fast I was dazed. Then the cabin was deserted save for Morgan and the guard. In a flash I was over the doorsill and in the cabin. Either I made a slight sound or the guard had intuition, for he half turned his head as my rifle butt crashed against his temple. He toppled from the stool.

Ben and I sprang toward Morgan. His eyes were wide with surprise. Fumbling in my haste, I struggled to cut the tough strips of birch bark around his hands. Ben removed the gag. He was about to cut the bonds around the ankles when Big Dan whispered hoarsely, "Look out! Somebody's coming back."

We stood frozen in panic.

"Get rid of the Ranger quick," said Morgan coolly. "Down there. Root cellar. Noticed it hours ago." He nodded toward a trap door in the floor at one side of the cabin. He rolled on his back to conceal his unbound hands.

Opening the cellar door we flung the stunned guard into the darkness below, then, rifles in hand, scrambled after him. We were just in time. Straining an ear at the door, I heard a brief mumble of talk. Next, Hawknose shouted, "Come back here, all of you."

I wiped my sweating palms on my shirt and pressed my ear again to a small crack in the door above, but I couldn't hear what was said. Big Dan must be lying his head off; as yet they had no suspicion of the root cellar.

There was another long wait. A dozen times I was on the point of raising the trap door and rushing out to pull a trigger and then go for them with knife and tomahawk, but common sense prevailed.

The situation was resolved for us. The stunned Ranger we had all but forgotten gave a loud groan. I groped for him, thinking to rip a piece off my shirt and cram it in his mouth. Before I could reach him he loosed a yell that could have been heard half a mile away.

A shaft of light fell into the darkness as the door was flung back. A body hurled itself at me. I shot from the hip and got a Ranger. An Indian screamed as Ben knifed him. Unfortunately, the door was wide enough to admit two at a time, and they came fast, throwing themselves on top of each other—and on top of us. We fought back as best we could, hacking, kicking, pounding, but in that small confined space it wasn't enough. Still fighting, we were hauled up to the cabin floor.

As I struggled to keep from being bound Hawknose cried in alarm, "Get him! His hands are free!"

Morgan had somehow raised himself in spite of his tied ankles and made a tremendous hop toward the leader. Three men threw themselves on him. He went down. There was a great uproar of threshing and thumping and cursing. In the end they trussed him up again.

I couldn't understand why there were so many of them left until I realized that the Ranger and Indian who had been sent to fetch Hawknose had returned. Counting the guard we had thrown into the cellar, who looked groggy, and an Indian Ben had slashed on the arm, seven of the gang were still present. Ben seemed half dazed. Breathing hard, completely helpless, I lay staring dully at the roof beam of the cabin.

The man known as Tremaine spoke. "We will settle this thing at once. There is no more time for bargaining. Dawn is here. Morgan, it may not be necessary to torture you. Matters have changed. I have two of your men. If you do not immediately agree to write that note I will have their throats cut—here, before you. If, after that, you are still stubborn, I will set these Indians to work on you. They are experts."

Big Dan was silent. The other waited.

"You blackguard," growled Morgan. "I'll write the message if you will set these young men free and send it by them to General Gates."

The other snorted impatiently. "You have a low

opinion of my intelligence. Free them to bring your pack yelling after me?"

Morgan, propped against the wall, was granite-faced.

"It is getting light," said Hawknose. "For the last time—" He broke off and spoke to a Ranger, who said something to the Indians in their tongue. They yelped with pleasure. Two of them drew knives and squatted beside Ben and me.

"One minute only," said Hawknose.

The edge of a knife was against my throat. I felt the chill dread of death.

"Bring the pen and paper," sighed Morgan.

A rifle cracked. In the small space of the cabin the sound was tremendous. The Indian beside me jumped to his feet convulsively, then fell across me.

With a scream of rage Hawknose sprang at Morgan, knife in hand. Another rifle stabbed flame from the window. The bullet caught Hawknose in mid-jump. He fell heavily at Morgan's feet.

The door burst open. With a ululating war cry Mike tomahawked an Indian. Caleb clubbed a Ranger. Jean Claude's rifle butt met Scarface's knife-wielding charge. Jerry and Pete Burns slid in over the window-sill. John Ray charged in through the door.

In a minute of crashing, grunting, deadly melee it was over. The surprise was complete. An Indian dashed from the door into the forest. The rest lay on the cabin floor. There were no wounded enemies to attend to.

Jerry set me free. "Lord a'mighty, Dave," he half

sobbed. "I thought he was cuttin' your throat. Had to shoot fast."

Myself, I was dazed—and suddenly filled with an amazed gratitude. "You did it, old friend," I muttered.

Ben and I shakily got to our feet. Morgan was sitting rubbing his ankles to restore circulation. "I'm getting too old to be tied up all night, specially this cold time of year," he grumbled.

The attackers had come out of the fight with surprisingly little damage. Jean Claude had a slash across a forearm. Pete Burns had been knifed in a shoulder. Caleb applied a tourniquet to Jean Claude's arm and expertly bandaged Pete's wound.

Morgan was standing, legs apart. "I don't know how you did it," he said. "But you did it right well. Did it mighty fine. Without you the three of us here would have been done away with by these skunks. Well, they won't do anybody any more damage. We owe you much."

He glanced around the cabin. His eyes dwelt malevolently on the figures of the two leaders, those ruthless, grasping men who at last had overreached themselves.

"I'll send some folks to clean up this place," he muttered. "Me, I never want to see it again. Let's get out."

It was the way we all felt. Without a backward look we walked out of the cabin into the gray light of a new day.

18

THE TURNING POINT

From force of habit we started out cautiously, silent and watchful. But our curiosity was too great. After a while Ben couldn't stand it any longer. "See here, fellows," he blurted, "how did you find us?"

Jerry glanced warily at Morgan, who appeared to be immersed in gloomy thought.

"It's all right," said Big Dan. "Don't worry about Indians and Rangers now. You boys took care of that. It's almost over. I'm mighty curious about the thing myself. Speak up, Gordon, you and Donaldson were there first. How did you find the place?"

I related the story as briefly as possible, for I was impatient to know how the others had gotten there so opportunely. For their benefit, I told how we had tried to free the Colonel and had been trapped in the root cellar.

"It was clever of those devils," growled Morgan. "To think I was ambushed like any blundering lobster-back!" He swore scornfully at himself. "The Indians we

243

ran into earlier must have been part of the gang. Haven't I learned anything since Braddock's defeat? We fought hard but I reckon I was pole-axed like the wounded man said. My God, and me trying to teach you how to fight in the woods! I'm a lunkhead!"

From Morgan, so often intolerant of others' failings, this was painful. Humility didn't suit him. I wanted to shut him up.

"It's the turn of those who got us out of this to tell how they did it," I said. "Jerry and Caleb and the rest."

After a short silence, Jerry spoke. "It 'minds me of the feller who went lookin' in the woods for his black dog at midnight. Looked rest of the night and never did find the dog. Well, we'd have had about as much chance as him if it hadn't been for pure luck. Now that's somethin' to think about—the part luck plays in things. I remember a feller who was said to be the unluckiest man in five counties. Nothin' ever went right for him and—"

"Get back on the subject," I implored, for Jerry evidently was in one of his rambling moods.

He gave me a hurt look. "Don't be so impatient," he complained. "All right. You remember Caleb and Mike and Jean Claude and me took off to the·north when we parted company with you. We went on that way for quite a piece until we met some New Hampshire militia. They hadn't seen no riflemen, let alone the Colonel. So we turned back and headed more west. Dark came on and we decided to stop for the night. That's where the luck started."

Much later, Jerry continued, they had heard someone threshing around in the brush. He and Caleb dif-
fered on the time this had happened—whether around
midnight or before. They couldn't see stars through the
overcast. They lay in wait, ready for anything, as the
sounds came nearer. Fortunately, they challenged before acting. They found out the sounds were made by
Pete Burns and John Ray, the ones who had started
back to camp with the wounded man. They had carried
him about a mile when the poor fellow died.

"That's how we met up with them and heard about
the ambush," Jerry went on. "They figured if Dave and
Ben caught up with that crowd there might be trouble
before they could go all the way to camp and come
back for help. So they thought to try to follow you in
spite of the dark. And we did the same."

"We were just going by a general sense of direction,"
put in Pete. "Turned out we weren't far off, but we
never would have picked up the trail you made if it
hadn't been for him." He nodded toward Mike. "I
swear he can see in the dark good as I can in daylight.
Can't you, Mike?"

Mike grinned. "Broken twigs were a big help. But
we lost the trail just the same."

So they had—and had been wandering around in a
forsaken way when they heard the firing that had
startled the gang some time after Hawknose had sent
the Ranger and Indian with the message to Burgoyne.
They had investigated but had found nothing to account for it. By instinct they had turned back, feeling
their way through the woods. Still later, they had seen

a faint light show for a moment to the west, as if a door
had been opened and shut.

"That must have been when the two who had been
sent for Hawknose came back late in the night, before
that bunch found us in the cellar," I said.

"Could be," replied Jerry. "Don't know about that.
Anyway, it was getting nigh dawn. We kept on until,
at first light, we made out the cabin. So then we laid
our plans and crept up on the place. I reckon that's
about it. I found the window open and saw the Injuns
ready to knife you. Scared the lights out of me."

"It didn't affect your aim," I told him thankfully.

We went on in silence for a time, each occupied by
his own thoughts. My chief thought was that it certainly was good to be alive. Then my mind turned to
Morgan's situation. It was intolerable that the man
who had made us into the best fighting corps of the
army, the man who had become a legend alike to
Americans and to the British and their auxiliaries,
should have his hard-won fame tarnished by one small
slip—by merely getting ambushed, which could happen to the most careful woodsman. Dan Morgan must
not be snickered at by belittlers, of whom every army
has a full share. Struck by an idea, I halted.

"Colonel, may I ask a favor?"

"Yes, Gordon," replied Morgan glumly. "If I can
grant it. You sure deserve it."

I bumbled in my search for words. "I—it's just—
just this. I think I can speak for every man here.
There's no reason anybody outside this little bunch
need ever know what happened yesterday and last

night. We can all swear to keep it quiet." I stopped, fearing I had hurt his feelings.

"That's a great idea, David." Caleb's voice was appreciative.

Morgan stared at me in astonishment. Slowly his rugged, tanned face flushed a deeper color. He shook his head. "Thank you kindly. You mean well. If I did that I would be denying all of you the credit that's your right. I can take my medicine."

The thought had fired the men's imaginations. They all started talking at the same time. *"Magnifique!"* exclaimed Jean Claude. "Come on, Morgan, promise," cried John Ray. "Chief keep big name," contributed Mike. "We'll do it anyhow," cried Ben.

Caleb stilled the clamor with upraised hand. "Colonel, it's not your personal reputation we're thinking about, or any credit you deem we should have. It's for the sake of the American cause. Think about it. Your very name is dreaded by the enemy. They're scared stiff of you. If anything happened that would cast the slightest shadow of doubt about us being invincible it could do a lot of harm to this army, to General Washington, and to all America. Besides," he added, "you're taking it too seriously. It could happen to the best scout ever born. Let's think of the greater gain."

"Hurrah!" we yelled.

Big Dan looked doubtful.

"Come on, men," said Ben. "Repeat after me: 'I swear I will never tell another living being what happened in these woods the afternoon and night of the thirteenth and fourteenth of October, 1777, so help me.' "

We did.

Morgan stood silent, rubbing his chin reflectively. On his countenance was an expression of humility such as I had never seen before. He tried to speak but choked up. Finally he got it out. "You—you. Well, blast it, you're my boys," he said, and stopped.

We all felt uncomfortable. I was near to tears, more from the strain of the night than anything else.

It was clever Jerry who broke the spell. "We got him, fellers. Now he's got to treat us nice. No more bellerin' and swearin' at us."

Morgan snapped out of it. Suddenly he gave Jerry a broad unaccustomed grin. "McGuire," he said, "one of these days I'm going to skin you alive."

When we reached camp we found the men there happy and triumphant. Burgoyne was getting ready to surrender, they told us. A deserter had disclosed that he had held a council with the German General von Riedesel and his other ranking officers. They had persuaded him to give up. There was no choice. An hour or so past a British officer had met Gates's aide, Wilkinson, had been blindfolded and conducted to headquarters. He had presented Burgoyne's terms for surrender. Gates had promptly pulled from his pocket his own terms.

All this had happened while we had been slipping through the woods and getting ourselves into trouble, out of touch with affairs. Burgoyne's offer indicated that he had not received the message about Morgan being held hostage. Perhaps the messengers had been waylaid; that could be the explanation of the firing we had heard. Morgan sent scouts to find the groups still combing the woods and bring them back. He then reported to Gates. We hoped he could keep his mouth shut. He did.

Militiamen had gone on holiday. They poured past our camp throwing their hats in the air and shouting: "We licked Burgoyne! Yankee doodle dandy! Now we can go home."

Cheered though we were, we viewed them sourly. "Summertime soldiers," muttered Jerry. "*They* licked Burgoyne, sez they, and now they can run back to pappy and mammy."

"They did their part," I said. "At least a lot of them showed up of their own free will when they were badly needed."

It was Caleb who got to the heart of the matter. "Without us and the Continentals it's hard to tell how much good their showing up would have done. Might have run when the pressure got heavy or might not have. Can't tell. But they added to our numbers and that was important. Because, you see, this is the turning point of the war. If we hadn't stopped Burgoyne, the British and their hirelings and the Tories might have worn us down. But not now. It's a long way from finished, but I tell you, this is the turning point."

"You think France may come to our help?" asked Jean Claude eagerly.

"After this, we can very likely count on it. We have

a smart old man as emissary to Paris—name of Benjamin Franklin, a Boston lad who went to Philadelphia for some reason and did all right in spite of that. He's been working hard persuading the French King and his advisers to come in on our side. This ought to convince them. The British won't have the run of the seas any more because the French have a good fleet. And they'd be glad to settle scores with the English for taking Canada and whipping them in India as well."

"It is good," sighed Jean Claude contentedly.

Our enthusiasm was dampened slightly during the next two days by developments. One was that Burgoyne was bargaining. After studying Gates's terms, he demanded a "Convention," which as near as we could make out meant not the complete surrender demanded by Gates but an agreement that his troops would be given the honors of war and sent back to England in British ships. To everybody's surprise Gates readily agreed.

The later result was that the Continental Congress overruled him. In the end the Britishers were held quite a time in Cambridge, where they and the Yankees didn't get on at all well. As for the Germans, they were finally sent down to Virginia, where General Riedesel and his family became friends of Thomas Jefferson and his wife.

The other development was bad news that came at this point from Philadelphia. General Washington's troops had lost a battle at Germantown, not far from the city. It seemed the British might even capture the capital.

"Oh, oh," groaned Jerry. "Now we're in for it. No rest for the weary. We'll be leavin' here soon, trust Dan for that. It's a long way to Philadelphy, and he'll run our tongues out a-gittin' there."

The morning of October 17, 1777, was pleasantly warm and still. By arrangement, Wilkinson rode alone to the British camp and witnessed the stacking of their arms in a small valley just north of the Fishkill where no other American eyes could see their shame. Then Wilkinson, with Burgoyne, General Phillips, General von Riedesel, and other high-ranking officers and their aides rode south to the Americans, where General Gates with his staff met them.

We were nearby and could see what happened. Burgoyne was wearing one of his splendid uniforms. Gates was in a plain blue smock. The two bowed and saluted each other. The British and German officers were introduced to the Americans. Then the two parties rode to the marquee that was Gates's headquarters.

Morgan formed us in two lines on either side of the road. To the north, regiment after regiment, 13,000 men in all, formed similar ranks facing the road as far as we could see, and beyond. Many were in Continentals; most of the militia were in plain farmer's clothes. But all stood stiffly, silently, gun butts on the ground.

Soon we heard from a distance fifes and drums shrilling and thumping "The British Grenadiers." But it didn't sound inspiring the way it had at St. Johns. The musicians' hearts weren't in it now. Then the first of the British appeared over the crest of the hill. They were light infantrymen and were led by a colonel. Their faces were grim. Some of the younger officers were quietly weeping. Their files marched by us defiantly. Others followed, and at last came the Germans, with women folk and bedraggled camp followers at the end. Some farmers from the neighborhood cursed the enemy, but the American ranks stood stiff and silent.

Thus passed into captivity 5,791 men—all that was left of the magnificent army that had set out from Ticonderoga in July to split the colonies, and win the war.

Burgoyne and Gates, with their officers, came out of the marquee where they had had dinner. Burgoyne unbuckled his sword and handed it to Gates. They spoke a few words, shook hands, and Gates returned the sword.

We broke ranks and clustered in a semicircle, watching. Burgoyne said something to Gates. The latter beckoned to Morgan. "Colonel," he called, "General Burgoyne wishes to meet you."

Big Dan strode forward. His faded field uniform contrasted with Burgoyne's splendor. But Morgan could be courtly when he wanted to be. He inclined his head as he shook hands. Burgoyne eyed him with curiosity. Then his gaze swept over the bunch of us.

"Colonel, I wanted to tell you," said Gentleman Johnny, with his actor's grace, "that you command what is probably the finest regiment in the world."

"Thank you, General. That was kindly put." Our Colonel turned his head and looked at us with an expression that seemed to me one of both amusement and pride, but mostly pride.

"Yes, General, they are right good soldiers—and they are mighty fine men," said Daniel Morgan.

The Author

ALLAN TAYLOR has been writing, in one form or another, since his graduation from Vanderbilt University. He has been a newspaperman on the Atlanta *Constitution*, the Atlanta *Journal* and is now with the New York *Times*. Among his six books are four works for young people. He has traveled widely through Europe and South America and spends his leisure time reading history, biographies and whodunits.

Mr. Taylor has two children and makes his home in New Jersey with his wife, who has co-authored several books with him.